Praise for *My Nem*

"Many have tried to give us an unreliable narrator; few have succeeded as well as Craig does . . . Tessa is a brilliant cross between the autobiographical fiction of Rachel Cusk and the untrustworthy narrator Charles Kinbote in Vladimir Nabokov's *Pale Fire*. Her narration is revealing and not; her pomposity is porous, funny." —*Boston Globe*

"A study of power dynamics and the roles individuals play in greater systems . . . Tessa is a Camus-obsessed misanthrope who has a thorny relationship with her daughter and a penchant for poking figurative bears, and yet in Craig's hands she's a mesmerizing narrator—even as she gets things wrong again and again." —*Vanity Fair*

"Craig has swapped the more lyrical, meandering prose of *Miss Burma* for a crisper style that carries a distinctly Cuskian chill. Tessa's tone is confessional but unapologetic, and the prose propulsive but pared back. What begins as a cautionary tale warning of the dangers of that bone-chilling phrase 'my feminism'—and just to be clear: my emphasis is on the first word—morphs into a much more multi-faceted and challenging story of the destruction of the lives of everyone involved." —*Financial Times*

"The book explores what it means to be feminine, a feminist, how we perceive these qualities, and how much our identities and beliefs define us. This book is short, sharp, philosophical, and dramatic. It's insightful and uncomfortable." —*Condé Nast Traveler*

"Craig's narrative is masterful and self-assured. Artful in its prose and unsparing in the way it looks at envy and its corrosive effects, *My Nemesis* is a riveting novel about the stories people tell themselves to justify their shortcomings and what happens when they start to believe these lies."

—*Alta*

"Charmaine Craig elegantly wrestles with the notion of rivalry between women in *My Nemesis*, an erudite novel about a woman in love with another woman's husband . . . Craig's literary talents cannot be denied in this thoughtful examination of rivalry between women, class differences and empathy." **—*Newcity Lit***

"The complicated relationship between memoirist Tessa and professor and philosopher Charlie becomes an entry to a layered exploration of the perception of the self and the outside world . . . A simple plot summary cannot capture the depth of Craig's treatment of such big themes as femininity and masculinity, motherhood and fatherhood, friendship and love . . . Craig offers an effective inquiry into the elusive nature of intimate relationships, whether they stem from love or hate." **—*Booklist* (starred review)**

"An intense portrayal of an intellectual affair as well as a private competition between two women with perfectly balanced moments of tension and introspection . . . Craig never lets her first-person narrator off the hook . . . Cerebral and tense." **—*Kirkus Reviews***

"A swift and cutting examination of rivalry between two women . . . The writing is biting and propulsive as allegiances shift . . . This confident work is sure to spark conversations."
—*Publishers Weekly*

"I devoured this sly, seething novel. So marvelously perceptive, so effortlessly elegant, it lays bare the horror of what husbands and wives expect of each other. *My Nemesis* is a pearl cultivated in justified rage. I loved it."
—**Sarah Manguso, author of *Very Cold People***

"Charmaine Craig's brilliant anatomization of mid-life art, identity, and infidelity shares in the intellectual grace and precision of its characters' philosophical pursuits, yet beneath the ruminative surface this book churns with desire and remorse."
—**Jonathan Lethem, author of *The Arrest***

"As deeply empathic as it is thrillingly addictive, *My Nemesis* is a stunning and brave literary feat. Charmaine Craig's searing prose and complex vision challenges us to abandon the safety and certainty of our own perspectives. What begins as a novel of female rivalry quickly transforms into a profound spiritual meditation on the danger of our inability—or unwillingness—to imagine and dignify the inner life of the other. With luminous grace, Craig's writing is a testament to the transcendent power and peace possible when we dare to try."
—**Fatima Farheen Mirza, author of *A Place for Us***

"*My Nemesis* is an exhilarating act of defiance, a novel that lights a match and sends the whole question of female characters' likability up in flames. Charmaine Craig is a writer unafraid of contradictions—at once elegant and unruly, cool yet searing—and here she's given us a fiercely philosophical novel that is also irresistibly, addictively readable."

—Sarah Shun-lien Bynum, author of *Likes*

"Charmaine Craig's *My Nemesis* is a spellbinding highwire act . . . a brutal exposition of the destructive underside of desire and the fragility of familial bonds. Craig's cutting sentences reveal how easily the life of the mind, sublime and addictive, can be transformed into a weapon that decimates lives. Perhaps most brilliantly, *My Nemesis* is a warning against the quiet grafting of racial power dynamics onto our most intimate networks of love. *My Nemesis* is a riveting clear-eyed burn of a book. Read it now!"

—Azareen Van der Vliet Oloomi,
author of *Savage Tongues*

"I was bowled over by this brilliant narrative of desire, complicity, and the limits of empathy. *My Nemesis* is a compact masterpiece in the confessional mode, one that reverberates long after the last page is turned. Bravo!"

—Antoine Wilson, author of *Mouth to Mouth*

"A blisteringly smart novel about feminism, identity and desire that refuses easy answers and will linger for a long time in my mind." —Monica Ali, author of *Love Marriage*

MY
NEMESIS

Also by Charmaine Craig

Miss Burma
The Good Men

MY
NEMESIS

A NOVEL

CHARMAINE CRAIG

Grove Press
New York

With special thanks to Htet Htet for sharing her story; to Mimi, Catherine,
Arthur, and Judy for the sanctuary; and to Andrew, Ellen, and Peter
for all their help with this.—C.C.

Published simultaneously in Canada
Printed in Canada

This book is set in 11 pt. Berling
by Alpha Design & Composition of Pittsfield, NH.

First Grove Atlantic hardcover edition: February 2023
First Grove Atlantic paperback edition: January 2024

Library of Congress Cataloging-in-Publication data is available for this title.

ISBN 978-0-8021-6270-0
eISBN 978-0-8021-6072-0

Grove Press
an imprint of Grove Atlantic
154 West 14th Street
New York, NY 10011

Distributed by Publishers Group West

groveatlantic.com

24 25 26 27   10 9 8 7 6 5 4 3 2 1

To Andrew

For there is merely bad luck in not being loved; there is misfortune in not loving. All of us, today, are dying of this misfortune.

—A.C.

Here there is *sickness*, beyond all doubt, the most terrible sickness that has thus far raged in man:—and whoever is still capable of hearing (but one no longer has the ears for it today!—) how in this night of torture and absurdity the cry *love* resounded, the cry of the most longing delight, of redemption in *love*, will turn away, seized by an invincible horror . . .

—F.N.

MY
NEMESIS

1.

WHEN I ACCUSED WAH of being an insult to women—
"an insult to womankind" was my unfortunate
phrase—we were sitting with our husbands at a fashion-
able rooftop restaurant in downtown Los Angeles. It was
late, I'd made the mistake of starting in on a third martini,
and straightaway I could feel the husbands begin to cower,
whereas Wah confronted me with a look of hurt, almost to
tell me that I'd betrayed some sort of feminine understanding.

"You've misunderstood me, Tessa," she said, and I noticed
that she was panting as though I'd shaken her physically. She
cast around for help from her husband, Charlie, whose steady
gray eyes were moving between us.

"I think not," I said, before he could save her.

But, of course, she had a point.

I'd never been able to read Wah, and I still don't believe
that it was a matter merely of culture or ethnicity. True, as

our current ethos would have it, she was a "person of mixed race," something that might have contributed, beyond her unusual look, to the confusion of her submissive and queen-like demeanor. Though I don't think even her relatives could have told you if her general mode of quietness was due to a timidity on her part or a righteousness that kept her at a remove from others; I don't think anyone knew if she tended to smile courteously during conversations with that supple mouth of hers because she was incapable of keeping pace with our ideas or privately counting the ways those ideas were imbecilic. What I'm trying to get at is that I found her to be a tangle of both deference and hostility, if also some beauty, which is why, before the restaurant incident (and my unfortunately phrased accusation), I was sympathetic when Charlie suggested he wanted to leave her.

His first letter to me, routed by email through my publisher about nine months prior to all this, was a response to my essay on the question of Camus's relevance. It's not often that I allow myself to feel flattered by appreciative words from readers; I think, if you are honest with yourself, you will agree that flattery should be allowed to mean something primarily to the flatterer. But with the first lines of Charlie's admiring letter, I understood that our minds could keep a certain, rare company. I soon broke my policy of not googling people whose work intrigues me, and after some searching I saw that he was a decently published philosophy professor at a research university near L.A. and, by any contemporary metric, practically invisible online. There was just one photo of him, on his department website: a candid-looking shot of an approachable, disheveled, frankly sexy man of middle age. Understand me: my swift response to his letter wasn't a matter of loneliness, sexual or otherwise; my husband of seven years, Milton, and I still enjoyed various forms of camaraderie, but when a darkly attractive man from a similar desert of intellectual isolation comes bearing a cup of consolation, one drinks!

Because Milton was semiretired by the time Charlie came into our lives, and because the last of our children from previous marriages had long before left our Brooklyn home, Milton and I had come to enjoy a life of resolute drifting between the city and his family farmhouse upstate. It was at the farm, as we called it, that I tended to receive Charlie's subsequent messages, which—for more reasons than I then understood—I began to share lavishly with Milton over our evening bottle of chilled wine. Any romantic union benefits from its share of excitements and threats; I suppose part of me thought it wise to remind Milton that others—in this case, a particularly eloquent, impassioned, and handsome man— could fall in love with, at least, my brain. But Milton found his own solace in Charlie's letters, with their comedic disclosures and humbly put insights. Milton's decision to phase out of the world of investment banking had been based largely on his desire to cultivate his passion for photography, a passion that was withering in inverse proportion to the amount of time he gave it, while, in his letters, Charlie complained of dying from a lack of scholarly productivity, a "sickness" caused by an inability to exorcise from his system everything he had come to understand yet couldn't write. Soon enough, in my replies to Charlie, I was quoting Milton's jocular retorts and bits of sympathetic advice, only occasionally feeling shouldered to the side by their developing male bond. We were three, to be sure, but none of us would have denied that I was the glue that made us three stick.

I see I've neglected to mention how the fourth among us fit into all this. Of course, from fairly early on in our correspondence, I'd learned of Charlie's nearly twenty-year marriage to Wah, of her lectureship position in Asian studies at his university, and of her one book, a work of nonfiction that told the story of a girl sold by her Burmese family to Malaysian child traffickers before her eventual transfer to the United States as an adolescent refugee. I'll admit that I frequently found myself violating my googling policy in those days, and I soon learned that Wah's prose (ignored in the few critical reviews of her book that I found online) revealed a certain intellect, whereas her author portrait displayed all the features of dependency and insecurity that my feminism urges me to decry: the wide, wounded gaze; the helpless fragility. Other online photographs showed her clutching at a thin, lost-looking girl: this was Htet, the subject of her book and, as Charlie told me, their now fifteen-year-old adopted daughter, "the fixed point of Wah's life." In a sense, it was because of Charlie's obligation to this relatively new familial arrangement, if not specifically to Htet or Wah, that I began to accept invitations to speak in California—that is, to give the kind of paid public readings and lectures there that since my marriage to Milton I'd had the privilege of generally turning down. You see, Milton and I were both eager to spend time with Charlie, who claimed to be able to get away only when a conference took him east. So it was that for a short period, Milton and I became regular houseguests at the Craftsman that Wah had meticulously restored in their rapidly gentrifying neighborhood in urban L.A.

Let me skip ahead, for a moment, to give you a picture of what life looked like then, when we were all briefly settled into this domestic scene; I mean, when Milton and I stayed at the Craftsman over the course of three or four visits, and Charlie and Wah took care to host various dinner parties for us, and Wah seemed always to be hovering at the edges of things, floating from room to room in one of her too-floral dresses while administering to our needs—unless she was attending to Htet, who only ever emerged to make some claim on her time. With all her capable subservience and her tolerance of the girl, it was almost as though Wah wanted to prove a point: that she was alone, not just in the

5

production of hostessing or parenting, but in the production of their shared life, and that her aloneness both explained her tragedy as Charlie's wife and ennobled her, for she was strong enough to bear it. But I'm getting ahead of myself, referring to Charlie's difficulties with Wah and the girl, when what I want is to give a glimpse of how things looked before all the trouble between us got going.

There was one night when it could have gone another way—not Charlie's situation, necessarily, but my own trouble with Wah, and no doubt her own trouble with me. It was after a party at the Craftsman, when the dinner guests had left. Everyone but Charlie and I had gone up to bed, and the two of us had embarked on one of the talks that typically stretched to dawn, talks that, though they left me decimated, I had come to crave, because through them we seemed to be nearing a precipice on the other side of which we might find the relief of having sorted out everything: the meaning of our marriages, of parenthood, of heartache and selfishness and all the rest of it. We were in the living room, sunken into the shabby armchairs that Charlie had made a point of telling me once belonged to his immigrant Jewish Romanian great-grandparents. It occurs to me that those chairs were the only part of that house that distinctly reflected and belonged to him. Well, he'd put on a single lamp—an old banker's lamp, by the looks of it, something that I imagined Wah must have found at an architectural salvage shop and whose ivory glass shade imparted a milky quality to the scant light. The near darkness was conducive to what Charlie and I were doing, it seemed to me, as if the boundaries not only between but also distinguishing us had been blurred, so that I wasn't always sure it was precisely *Charlie* whom I was addressing or precisely me, *Tessa*, chasing a perilous thought. We were discussing the question of whether a writer should still be read if in life he had proved to be a monster (should I still be read if with this confession I seem sometimes to be one?), and as the darkness enfolded us more completely, I felt Charlie retreat into a silence so absorbing I thought he might have drifted off. And for an illicit moment, I sat in the intimacy of that silence, imagining his awkwardly long body stretched out on the chair, so close to mine.

"I can't write about him anymore," I heard myself instructing the silence, as though to argue myself out of something. We had been speaking of Camus—or I had been doing so, while Charlie had fallen silent. "I think of his wife, his daughter, all the women he pledged himself to and yet misled and damaged."

But even as I said this, a sensation came over me, that of being hounded like a small animal chased into a hole, or rather of being a small animal bounding for a hole in which was buried its own guilt, and the problem was to get to the guilt and bury it still deeper before my capture. What was this transference? Wasn't I innocent, allowing myself only the freedom to flirt a bit with Charlie when we'd all had a few drinks, never transgressing on anything more than his time or his mind? I was a faithful wife to Milton, a competent (if flawed) mother to a daughter who was at that moment studying law in order to work for the social good. Why should I feel implicated by the very process of standing in judgment of my literary master?

It must have been three or four hours later when, with a jolt, I became aware of a noise in the kitchen: running water and a gentle clattering that told me Wah was cleaning up. Charlie's chair was empty now, someone had tucked a blanket around me, and it was lighter out, near dawn. I had the thought to throw off the blanket and slip upstairs, but that same terrible feeling of guilt kept me in my chair, and another half hour must have passed.

When I finally gathered courage to go into the kitchen with the blanket wrapped around my shoulders, I found Wah doing the dishes in her robe. She seemed to have expected me and dried her hands, crossed to the small blue teapot she liked to use, and poured me out something hot and reedy. As I stood there awkwardly trying to sip it, she looked up at me as if wanting to say something, so that I wished I'd checked the mirror before exposing myself to her in my rumpled state.

"We're a burden to you," I said, to tell her that *she* was a burden, her stare, her sincerity.

"No," she said quietly. "It's better when you're here. When you're here, so is Charlie."

The admission was so plainly put, and it brought up so many questions—it seemed to implicate Charlie so terribly and yet so passively—that I wanted to rebel against it. I set my cup down on the counter, whose vintage tiles Charlie had told me Wah had taken tremendous trouble to source. And I said something about the tea being too bitter for my taste, which caused Wah to laugh, not condescendingly, only as though she found me amusing.

But it was with an air of sadness that she picked up my cup and set it in the sink and stared down at the thing before saying, "I was just thinking about your conversation last night with Charlie—it's impossible not to hear things when the house is quiet." The thought that she had listened to our private conversation—that she had listened to me—was only slightly less appalling than what she proceeded to say: "I was thinking about how when Htet was little, if she didn't come home with enough money at night, the traffickers beat her. Tied her up and deprived her of food. She had to sell trinkets on the street."

I had the vague sense that I was being likened to human traffickers. "I'm not sure what that has to do with our conversation," I said, not meaning to sound quite so cruel.

Wah squinted around at me from the sink. "I was thinking about your conversation *in light of* Htet," she said, speaking

9

very slowly. "I was thinking about Camus, his womanizing, and about Htet being strung up and whipped and sometimes raped. I'm not condoning what Camus did. I feel for his wife. It's just that I worry we're losing distinctions."

Well, you could relativize away just about any crime with Wah's reasoning, and hearing it, I should have regained my moral and intellectual advantage, not to mention salvaged some control over my facial expressions and racing pulse. But that senseless guilt rose up in me again, and stupidly I said, "I think you're not quite understanding what Charlie and I were debating—the question of whether or not an evil cancels out a good. Or if the two can be reconciled, regarded as part of the same continuum that still merits consideration."

Of course, that wasn't really what Charlie and I had discussed, and Wah must have known it. A small, worried scowl marred her brow. She might have been doing something as earnest as fretting for my soul. "Htet has taught me so much about that," she said. "When she was on the streets, an old man tried to get her to do things, 'weird things' is her way of describing it. He was rich, and whenever he approached asking for what he wanted, she would demand that he pay her up front. And as soon as she had the money, she would take off, and he'd just watch her escape. Over and over this happened—he gave her money, watched her escape. I'm telling you this because Htet says someday, when she makes enough money of her own, she'll go back and find this man and return everything she stole from him."

It was almost pleasurable, the indignation that coursed through my blood then. It seemed to absolve me, the little animal, bounding for my hole. "That's a horrific thing to say," I told her. "Horrific and misguided. And as her mother, you have a responsibility to correct her. To get her therapy instead of encouraging this harmful self-sacrifice."

She looked like she could cry then. "I know you have your reasons, Tessa," she said quietly. "But your reasoning is ordinary."

2.

Y OU HAVE ASKED ME to give an account of what trans-
pired before Wah's death. I realize there is little chance
of me coming off as blameless. Maybe that is your intention:
to make me see the cruelties—my cruelties—that exacer-
bated Wah's hurt, if not caused it outright. But witness my
little sketch of Wah in her kitchen, how cutting she could
be. Witness how she delivered her blows as if it caused her
physical anguish to wound me, as if the blows themselves
were a form of self-sacrifice. Aren't the actions of a bludgeon-
ing victim as despicable, spiritually speaking, as the hardness
of heart of which you have accused me?

I know I haven't returned to the restaurant incident
with which I started, yet there is nothing more painful to
a writer than being accused of ordinariness of mind, and if
this is also an exercise in reconcilement (as much as it is a
confession of meanness), then I must defend the thinking

that, after all, initially brought Charlie to me—brought him
to me because he found such solace in it. I am a memoirist who doesn't shy away from the political and theoretical
subjects that I find preoccupying, and on the surface, *Midlife*,
the rather philosophically minded book to which Charlie so
strongly responded, repurposes some of Camus's thinking
in his *The Myth of Sisyphus*. As you might imagine, Camus's
book, like mine, addresses the absurdities of middle age, with
death looming on one side, disappointment on the other, and
nothing but a Sisyphean wheel of activities supporting the
structure of one's present. "Rising, tram, four hours in the
office or the factory, meal, tram, four hours of work, meal,
sleep and Monday, Tuesday, Wednesday, Thursday, Friday and
Saturday," is how Camus puts it, which roughly translates
in contemporary (and yes, I know, Western, first-world, if
not necessarily "privileged") terms to: wake up, caffeine, harried morning interactions, work, meal, work, harried evening
activities, inebriated consumption of screen media, (occa-
sional) foggy sex, fitful sleep, repeat, repeat, repeat. Assuming
one *doesn't* have young children.

I am too cynical to reserve judgments, as you've no
doubt noticed, and you could say that my essay was written
from the perspective of a woman staring down into the abyss
of a cynicism that had become too gargantuan to tolerate.
There was the wreckage of my first marriage behind me.
There was the damage I had caused my daughter—damage

whose depths I was only beginning to fathom. There was everywhere the thickening atmosphere of hatred and injustice, in the face of which I could no longer claim to know the purpose of my writing, which broadly took aim at the ways men ensnare women (a preoccupation born of my first marriage), while solipsistically fixating on my own life. As Camus puts it, "One day the 'why' arises and everything begins." One either returns in a stupor to the slog or awakens, the consequence of the latter being "suicide or recovery." Now, the lure of wanting to blow up one's life was something to which Charlie could also relate. And it turned out that his hour of crisis, like mine, had been brought on by the shocks and shames of parenthood, as much as anything.

This isn't meant to be about *my* life—at least not apart from Wah's—but, after disparaging my tendency toward writerly solipsism, I'll take a moment to tell you about the daughter who led me to the precipice of my vertiginous abyss. Eleonore is brilliant, self-possessed, pleasant looking, preoccupied with justice, sometimes shy, moody, and self-isolating—all in a quiet, diminutive way. I think it's fair to say that we share a certain regard for each other while never having been particularly intimate. I can't remember a time when together we didn't resemble two polite adults rather than mother and child, a strained self-consciousness blooming between us with the divorce when she was eleven and we began to live together half-time—then less than half—then much less. She was thirteen when I met Milton, fourteen when I yielded to her request that she be left alone whenever I decamped to the farm along with Milton and his college-bound boys; she was fifteen when *she* decamped full-time to her father's place on the Upper West Side. I don't want to get into the business of gender and parenting, but Milton's brand of patience for adolescence had its influence on me. "Go ahead and leave her" was his general sentiment; for reasons selfish and feminist, I stifled my nagging counterargument that Eleonore was just a child, hardly more than a little girl, though I see now that it was also hurt that kept me silent when it came to her retreat. With Milton, I'd had the fantasy of starting a better, healthier period of motherhood. Instead, Eleonore had separated from me with an outsized independence that I told myself would serve her well in life.

My actual hour of crisis came when Eleonore was nineteen and spending her spring holiday from Sarah Lawrence with her father and his new, young family. We often corresponded by email, she and I, which was more natural to our relationship than the messiness of texting; I hadn't been the least put off when I received by email her request that we find time soon to have lunch at our favorite ramen place near Washington Square. But even before she spotted me emerging from the cotton panels separating the dim restaurant from the rainy street, I felt panic digging its claws into me. Eleonore was seated at a table at the far end of the constricted, mostly vacant interior, her eyes trained on a menu, her shoulders stiffening under the reproachful tension of her delicate neck. All at once, she turned the menu over, so that I knew she sensed my presence and was silently conveying her refusal to reassure me that all was well—that we were well. You see, during her adolescence, in addition to increasingly refusing to stay with me, she had sometimes shut down all lines of communication between us. This was done, I should say, in her nearly silent, avoidant manner, such that it often took me weeks to grasp that her customary remoteness was now complete and that I had invariably wounded her, though how those wounds were caused she never proceeded to tell me.

I'm aware of having something of a problem with laying blame. When you spend your life in consideration of human relations and your thoughts unavoidably chase down networks of behavioral causality, it's difficult to hold your tongue when your own blunders originate in others'. Still, even as I wielded my wet umbrella and rushed to the table where Eleonore persisted in her scrutiny of the menu, even as I planted myself down with a breathless "*Nora?*" and drew (not quite snatched) the menu from between her fingers, even then, I assure you, I was already chastising myself for doing harm to her willingness to see me—and harm to my own inner peace. I wasn't quite yet aware of how perilous her ongoing rejection of me had become—perilous for *me*—but the pain was right there under the surface, threatening to ignite that Sisyphean *why*, if not to extinguish my remaining faith in love, in parenthood, in life.

For an unnerving moment, she stared into my eyes, though there was no meaning in her stare; she seemed to be deliberately stripping meaning from the light waves passing between us. Only then, as I searched her slight features, did I see that she appeared less pale than wan, dazed. It was the same way she had looked as a child when she was coming down with something.

"You look well," I lied. I was so afraid of offending her.

Even this seemed to be an affront to her, as if it confirmed something tragic in her estimation of my being. She studied my face, her expression vacillating between resolution and hesitancy; she could have been deciding whether to forge ahead with whatever it was she meant to discuss or to give up on me forever.

I wasn't pleased when the waitress intruded on all this. And it was almost hurtful, if not surprising, the way Nora lit up with a smile for the woman, whom I recall being more interested in the paper on which she scrawled our orders than in returning Nora's courtesy. Yes, Nora was unstintingly polite, and something about her smile now—something about its innocence and generosity—broke my heart open. With it, I remembered the toddler in Prospect Park, eager to join in games at which she was never adequately adept, her already keen intelligence veering left where other children's seemed invariably to turn right.

"I've missed you," I said when the waitress departed. Which was true. "Terribly."

An indefinable sadness rose in Nora's eyes and, I imagine, a visible hope in mine. But a moment later her stiffness returned, and I saw that she was defending herself against another onslaught of disappointment in me. It had been stupid to say I'd missed her when I'd also been negligent about writing, visiting. Negligent and circumspect.

For a while, twenty or thirty minutes, we managed to find a path through the thickets of our difficulty. The ramen came, as did beers that I'd heedlessly added to our order by waving down our server and calling for two Asahis, something, I noticed, to which Nora didn't object. Then we sought recourse in the spiciness and the foam, stuffing our stunned mouths and dabbing our noses and eyes, as Nora said something about her roommate, and I said something about a trip Milton and I were planning to take (I wondered if I should invite her, though she would know the thought of including her hadn't previously occurred to me). When we finally relinquished our napkins, it was almost as though we'd arrived on the other side of a good shared cry.

But all at once it struck me that Nora wasn't so much sick or upset as chemically altered. *Pregnant*, I thought.

"Whatever is going on, Nora," I said, "here I am. Let's talk about it."

All the light that had risen to her face drained away. "Why do you do that?" she said, and, again, she fell into that measured scrutiny, as if she were trying to discover in my expression the answer to a question she dared not speak. "Why do you assume the problem with me is somewhere out there, somewhere far away?"

"You're making assumptions. I don't assume—"

"And why do you do that? Word games. Take my words and use them against me?"

"I have no idea—"

"But you think you do. You think you're all-knowing. You tell people you write about life. You're tired of make-believe. The make-believe of your first marriage. The make-believe of domestic harmony. The make-believe of liberated women. But *you're* the make-believe artist. You're the one living in the land of fantasy."

I suppose I couldn't sit there listening to her line of attack for another second. But I was also still a concerned mother. "Are you pregnant, Nora?"

The question plainly took her aback—and not for its acuity. No, my comprehensive wrongness was evident straightaway, something she only emphasized—relished— with a shake of her head and a scoff that verged on hysterics.

"I wish," she said now, "I really wish, that you were better at reading people. And at knowing how you make them feel. I had to read *The Divided Wife* in English class." *The Divided Wife* being my second book, the one about our pre-divorce lives.

"Is that what happened?"

"Can you imagine? Having to sit there and listen to your peers, your professor, talk about published misinterpretations of your own life? Misinterpretations that pretend to be truth with a capital *T*."

"You didn't tell the professor we're related?" I think by that point I was shouting, though she had hardly raised her voice.

"Why would I do that when I want people to see the real me?"

"I've only ever meant to represent *my* side, Nora!" Even then, in the interval during which I gasped for breath before my next utterance, I seemed to glimpse the immeasurable cruelty of my honest words. "*Myself*."

"That's just it, Mom. All you *care* about is your side. And you don't even know the reality of who you are."

21

3.

DOESN'T OUR THINKING—the *way* we perceive, the intimate hours of consciousness we spend only with ourselves—form the substance of our reality?

When I think now of Charlie's reality, or at least the reality he felt himself to be living when he first approached me, I see he was a man of exile, someone banished from the life he had been set up to live, or at least someone who had banished himself. And I might as well add that I sometimes wonder if his having a wife and child of a different race compounded that sense of not belonging. Of course, the thought may come from some access of envy, a wish that I had been the woman he called "wife." Though I see clearly that living with him must have also been a kind of torment for Wah.

I remember the time he let on that they were in trouble, a few months after his first letter to me, when a summer conference brought him east, and we convinced him to delay his return and stay the night with us at the farm. It's an odd thing to feel close to someone without ever having been in his presence—the opportunities for disappointment and embarrassment upon meeting are formidable. And as Milton and I stood in the shade of the rambling clapboard shaking Charlie's hand and then awkwardly embracing him, I was overtaken by a sort of violence of relief. Charlie's physical self—his skin and scent and tallness—met no resistance from my expectations and, instead, exceeded them. He was so extremely handsome, so clean smelling and long limbed, and the entire scaffolding of my composure crumbled under the weight of my physical self's response to him. I have no idea what any of us said during those first minutes; I remember only how we laughed, how even Milton turned pink with giddiness. I think Milton must have been grasping the same thing I was: that we'd pinned our obscure hopes on Charlie for reasons we hadn't yet named, and that we hadn't been foolish after all in granting this stranger entry into our lives.

As if to celebrate our collective relief and deplete ourselves of excitement, the three of us set straight out on a strenuous walk through the farm, skirting the spring-fed pond where I knew the afternoon sunshine and shade would still be coming in bursts and where I suspected Charlie—who had told me in a letter that he liked to swim and fish—would want to return. Soon we were standing at a little lookout point over the dusky greenhouse and a pasture where I thought someday I might keep sheep as Milton's grandfather had. I normally took tremendous joy in the vista, but maybe because of the heat and the mosquitoes I felt a sort of fraudulence overcoming me as I stood there catching my breath beside the men. I had the unpleasant thought that I'd done nothing to earn the right to claim the view as mine, nothing other than marry Milton, who for decades had poured money into the place in order to maintain it and who bore in his perpetually stunned expression all the evidence of his outsized sense of responsibility—including for me. I was almost embarrassed. But when I glanced around at Charlie and saw how easily his eyes roamed over the well-watered land—all the acres and acres that were ours—it occurred to me that he didn't appear to be the least bit at odds with what he saw. He seemed instead to have come into possession of something extraordinary himself, almost as though he were surveying his own recently acquired property.

Or maybe my memory has been tarnished by feminist revisionism, a retrospective anger that as he stared out over those fields, I couldn't see evidence in his expression of the trouble he'd left behind—of Wah and Htet and all the difficulties they faced. Do you think it's a male thing, the ability to see only what one happens to find relevant or pleasing in a moment, while women are left to keep track of the whole messy business of constructing the world behind that view? Truth be told, I didn't want to think of Wah that day. Throughout my correspondence with Charlie, I'd found it convenient that he'd kept his attachment to her mostly out of sight.

"Come whenever you want," I heard Milton say, and when I turned, I saw that he, too, was gazing over the farm with the purest look of satisfaction. It must have been a balm to him that Charlie was so genuinely taken by the place. It must have made what he had sacrificed for me seem almost justifiable.

Charlie cast an indistinct look at Milton. "I could use the refuge," he said.

The frankness with which he'd spoken seemed to disconcert Milton, but I saw he was also pleased to be able to help our new friend. "Whenever you want," he went on with a blush. "You can have the use of the guesthouse—or the barn if the kids are in town. And just write. Think and write. Let us take care of you now."

There's something in philosophy called "perspectivism." Charlie introduced me to the concept. He said it calls us not merely to consider other people's values and perspectives— that would be the politically correct thing to do—but to see the world as it is *constituted* by their values. When I think about it, those are profoundly different things. A framework like intersectionality suggests that making a perspectivist leap is not intuitive—and perhaps even impossible—because our circumstances, privileges, and disadvantages are so various. In my own field many would say, as in fact I have somewhat vehemently, that we possess neither the right nor the authority to write what we have not lived. From early on, I committed myself to the memoir form because I believed that, as far as experience goes, mine is all I have to go on and because I've felt that to write about others—imagined or "real"—is to participate in appropriation, not to mention lying. But here I am, a woman accused by her child of being ill acquainted with her own past and reality, a woman struggling to tell the story of people whose circumstances she has never shared—Wah and Htet and those I'll get to. And what I'm wondering is how high the walls of misunderstanding between us must become before we stand back and put our sights on each other's worlds. You would say *each other's souls*.

The night of Charlie's first visit, Milton served us a pasta dish at the farm table in the kitchen. Eating there had been my idea. I'd thought it would start things off on a more comfortable note. But I'd made the mistake of seating Charlie with his back to the French doors leading to the patio and pool area. Charlie has wonderfully expressive, direct eyes—they are very large, and there is a way he catches you with their gaze when he is making one of his impassioned points. Now that I think of it, he has something of Camus about him, what with those eyes and his combed-back hair and the impression he gives, despite his vulnerability, of being awake to his own charms. Yet that night, even as he fixed that mesmerizing gaze on us, his attention kept being drawn to the growing darkness behind him, as though a predator were somewhere on the loose out there and his brain were prompting his eyes to be more vigilant. I had the thought, when I saw that he chose to eat most of his meal with the teaspoon Milton had set down only for form, that the raw boy in him was very close to the surface of the man, and it struck me that he'd never told me about his childhood. For all I knew, he'd come from a hardship he had mostly learned to conceal. And for some reason I was reminded of the way my parents had prevented me as a child from intruding on their parties by insisting they were embarrassed by my smell, a contrivance that must have been the most effective measure their stunted imaginations and hearts could come up with.

But all the awkwardness fell away later, after dinner, when I took a bottle of wine by the neck along with two glasses and told Milton, who had already started washing up, to come join us when he was done around the other side of the house, on the deck overlooking the orchard and the woods beyond. It was a lovely evening, warm and touched by the humming of crickets and a soft breeze not unlike the one I would come to know in Wah and Charlie's neighborhood, albeit absent of the pollution. And with the wine and the continued strangeness of being together, Charlie and I sat alone like that for a time, not facing each other but looking out toward the greater night. It occurs to me that our best, most honest talks always took place in the shadows, as if we were a pair of filmgoers drawn by the darkness into a communal intimacy.

We'd been talking over dinner about what in *The Myth of Sisyphus* Camus calls "Don Juanism," something in *Midlife* I'd referred to as "womanizing," though I recognize these now as being qualitatively different—as different as Camus's world from mine. Camus says one way to commit suicide is to give the entire self to another, just the opposite of Don Juan's habit: "A mother or a passionate wife necessarily has a closed heart, for it is turned away from the world. A single emotion, a single creature, a single face, but all is devoured. Quite a different love disturbs Don Juan, and this one is liberating. It brings with it all the faces in the world." A very male sort of trick, you might say, this neutralizing of the damage wrought by male womanizing and this maligning of a woman's devotion—a devotion, I might add, that men like Charlie as much feel themselves owed as long to escape. Yet my desire to remain amorously engaged with the world has long caused me, too, to chafe against the pressure I've felt to give more entirely of myself in marriage and parenthood, and in *Midlife* I tried to grant a woman such as myself—one with the drive also to self-create—permission not to hang herself by the particular and *expected* rope of self-sacrifice.

On that warm night, out on the deck in the darkness with Charlie, drinking wine and listening to the susurrations of his breath, I had the thought that a sensitive, cerebral, ambitious man like him, a man who also happened to be a father and a husband, might find himself in need of just such permission.

"He's a fugitive," I heard him say, his sonorous voice rending the silence so that I was momentarily startled. Not until he went on did I understand that he was picking up the thread of our conversation over dinner and referring to Don Juan: "A lover with the freedom of a solitary, unattached man. And someone who's doomed to despair because his escape has no value, because he's not leaving any*one*."

I could hear, far away from us, the clanging of Milton putting away a pan, and for the first time I became conscious of the immense danger I felt myself to be in with Charlie. My mind kept playing tricks, perverting his words, words I wanted to read myself into, so that his last phrase became *because I'm not leaving you.*

"What you're talking about," I heard myself stammer, in a pitch no doubt meant to cut through his conviction, "what you're conjecturing—that, essentially, womanizing and male adventure only have excitement if there's a faithful woman standing by, a safe, pretty haven for the adventuring man to return to—it's male fantasy. It's Odysseus and Penelope redux. Would you say it was *reasonable* for Penelope to stay celibate for twenty years while he was off chasing his ego?"

When Charlie didn't immediately answer, my desperation to maintain his interest in me all at once vanquished my need to prove him wrong. It's always jarring for me to realize that the intoxicant of intellectual engagement can be dispelled for some people when they feel challenged or chastened. But, of course, we weren't engaging only in the intellectual realm. We were talking about love, about ourselves. We were talking about Charlie and Wah. And, anyway, the question of Penelope's reasonableness was beside the point, as celibacy had been her choice. For a moment, I was sure I'd made an unforgivable mistake, and I found myself resorting to another deep drink of wine.

But then he said, his voice a better, richer drink of reassurance: "I know it's not what you want to hear, Tessa. I know it's not what I'm *supposed* to say. Blame it on social programming, narrative clichés. Deride it. Wish it away. None of it changes the fact that I have needs, *as a man*."

"As do I, *as a woman*."

"Of course. And some of my needs, *as a man*, are for solitude and escape."

"Needs I can relate to having—*as a woman*."

31

"I'm not talking about womanizing, by the way. Don Juan isn't my hero. He's a sad figure because he lacks a romantic bond with some*one*, as I've said."

There it was again, his focus on "one," my dangerous mental wordplay—*I'm a sad figure because I lack a romantic bond with you.*

"But he also isn't a fool, Tessa, whatever you might think of him. He claims his freedom to roam, to quest, to duel, to strive on his own, all of which the modern family man is denied."

I should have said, *Like women of all times!* Or: *As if the family edifice wouldn't collapse if all parents were so selfish!* I think a part of me began to despise Charlie then. And yet, my heart battering against my chest, I held my tongue, because— because I caught a glimpse of myself in that selfishness.

"Does Wah make it difficult for you to travel?" I ventured, and in the darkness I felt embarrassment bloom on my cheeks. I was prying, no doubt because I wanted Charlie to divulge something ugly about his wife.

For a moment, I sensed him straining to see me, and I tried not to avert my face. It seemed possible he might more fully reveal himself. But it was with reproach that he said, "No one supports me more than Wah."

4.

I THINK IT WAS ON HIS NEXT VISIT to us, a few weeks before we finally traveled west and met Wah and Htet, that Charlie confessed to me that he'd never wanted children. The admission came after we'd dined in the city with Milton and my editor, who as it happens had recently become an older father. I'd so wanted to help Charlie with his writing. He was brilliant at connecting with people, and I'd felt sure my editor would be taken by him, if not able to steer him through the scholarly and creative impasse he felt he was in.

And the evening, though warm, had begun encouragingly enough, with my editor and Charlie bonding over the work of the German philosopher Feuerbach, a biography of whom my editor had published decades back, and whose formative critique of Christianity you're no doubt acquainted with. I don't think I'd grasped until then that Charlie has something of a metaphysical and old-fashioned streak in him.

We are living in purifying times, when people seek pared-down rights and wrongs, heroines and perpetrators standing in uniform, not complicated considerations of the belief systems that so often continue to divide us. I can't recall everything Charlie said over dinner—I remember him fixating on one of my least favorite woman haters, Nietzsche, whom he blasphemously claimed was as much critiquing the structure of misogyny as lamenting Christianity *and* its demise ("He even celebrated Christianity, considering it still the best answer we've come up with in response to the meaning of our suffering"). To my agitated ears, it almost sounded as though Charlie were sermonizing, excusing misogyny and bemoaning secularism; he certainly wasn't offering up commercially enticing, politically germane fare. And in the light of my editor's alert gaze, I began to recognize the growing darkness of dismay. "Enough about dead white men," Milton finally put in with a rescuing laugh. And then thoughtlessly: "Did you know Charlie is married to the writer Wah Weldon?"

Because Charlie had asked if we might return to the farm that night—"it's such a haven"—we made the long trek back upstate after dinner. I remember the silence of that car ride, with glazed Milton behind the wheel and Charlie looking lost on the air-conditioned seat behind him. I had the instinct to search the gloom beyond my window for something to claim my attention, to wrest it from an inner sense of dread. I so wanted to maintain my faith in Charlie—in his astuteness, including the astuteness of his belief in me. And yet, staring alternately at the night and my fatigued reflection in the glass, I had the feeling that inviting him into our lives had been a misstep after all, something doomed to disappoint and embarrass me. And I had the thought that I might have arranged the evening's dinner out of vanity as much as generosity; I'd been so sure that Charlie would flatter the self-portrait of the modern and culturally relevant woman that I suppose I'm continually striving to paint.

I have few friends, and I have justified this to myself by recalling to mind not only my private nature, but the demands of the writing life. Yet as I glanced back at Charlie in the rearview mirror and saw how alone he seemed, like a boy at the mercy of a cold world, I remembered that in one letter he'd mentioned his feeling that Htet "hated him," and it seemed to me that my own difficulty with a daughter—my difficulty spending time with Eleonore for the very reason that she encountered so much difficulty with me—was not unrelated to both my habit of self-isolation and my vanity. Where there is no one to intimately confront one, there is no one to judge one's ugliness and failings. Hadn't I left Eleonore's father because I could no longer stand the feeling that he hated me?

"You know," Charlie said when Milton had finally gone up to bed, and the two of us were facing each other in the humid shadows of the farmhouse living room, "I guess I should have gone with Wah to Malaysia to pick up Htet from the convent in Kuala Lumpur."

From various reviews of Wah's book, I understood that Htet had spent her last year in Malaysia at a series of juvenile shelters. I'd heard nothing about a convent, but something told me not to press Charlie now for explanations.

"I should have gone and seen it myself," he went on, rather miserably.

He adjusted himself on his seat, one of the claustrophobic sofas that Milton's boys insisted on keeping. In the dimness, I saw him cast several panicked glances over his shoulder, as if in anticipation of someone—perhaps Milton from the foyer—crashing through the concealment that we'd temporarily claimed. A tic, I thought, wanting all at once to turn on the lamp beside him, if only to cast out the unnerved boy and regain the attentive man.

"Not to write about it," he clarified. "I'm not in competition with Wah. But to see what Htet came out of, her world, the streets."

In his expression of regret, I couldn't help but notice the absence of an explicit mention of Htet's interests. Another father might have said he ought to have gone for Htet's sake, to welcome her into their family. I asked him why he had decided not to go, and the question seemed physically to disturb him, such that he shifted once more on his seat. But he appeared to regain his ease the moment I crossed toward him to finally switch on the lamp. Or maybe I was the one who became comfortable with him again; in the softly glowing light, all his boyish agitation resolved itself in the symmetry and soulfulness that made him so exceptionally pleasing.

"Do you think it's strange," he said, watching as I sat, "that Wah told me she wanted children only a few days after we met—before we were even together? She was only twenty-three."

"Strange to have known she wanted children?"

The truth is, I've never understood women like that, women who seem to be more result oriented with respect to their reproductive capabilities than romantic, as though Eros were, in fact, merely that clichéd means to a Darwinian end rather than a culmination in the great human quest for closeness and meaning. With Eleonore's father, Nick, whom I met as an undergraduate, there had existed only the abstract possibility of our starting a family, even after we married. And long before the realities of a child's purloining of my body and time had really exerted their entitlements over me, I was terrified by the news that we were expecting. For Nick, though, the pregnancy seemed to expel some burden he'd been carrying—the burden to prove himself an ideal husband, maybe, and the burden to realize his ambitions as an architect. You know, his reaction to fatherhood strikes me now as being almost "maternal" in the Camusian sense, devotional to the point of self-abnegation. Within weeks of Eleonore's birth, he'd given up on private practice and accepted a position with a New Jersey–based firm primarily commissioned to design shopping complexes; when I expressed dismay at this shortchanging of his vocational aspirations, he explained for the first (but not last) time in our relationship that the importance I granted self-expression was not necessarily something he could fully respect.

"I don't think it's unusual for certain women to go into adulthood with motherhood as an objective," I said to Charlie. It occurred to me that he and Wah must not have been able to conceive. "Conventional, yes. Suspect, perhaps."

My answer seemed to go down uneasily with him. He reached for the glass of wine that had been chilled when I'd poured it out and that had sat untouched since we'd sunk into our opposing seats; but he didn't raise the glass now to drink—he was too preoccupied with the defense of Wah forming behind his lips. "I'm not suggesting she was the first woman who'd mentioned wanting children to me," he said, so that I couldn't decide if he felt a certain pride about it, if he traced these women's want all the way down to the origin of their want for him. "But there was something about the way Wah said it. Until then, fatherhood had seemed like a toll I could possibly avoid paying. And then . . ."

"Then?"

"Bewitched."

"You poor thing."

He didn't seem to register my sarcasm. "She was so sincere," he said, as if he were really a victim of her sorcery. "And so soft, feminine."

Writing this, I'm reminded of an essay I was then struggling to piece together about the way nearly every brilliant woman I knew had involved herself in a long-term partnership with a petulant man, as if petulance in a male partner were a requirement if one didn't go in for obedience or emotional vacuity, or as if a woman's exceeding competence and reliability let a man off the hook emotionally or sabotaged his equanimity and strength. It could have been petulance—my own—that caused me to want to dismantle Charlie's absurd conception of his wife as a "feminine" fertility object. The sensation I had then was just the same as when I'd been young—five or six—and one of my neighborhood friends asked me to help her stone a crow. I had embarked on the task with guilt, yet also with faith in my friend's shrewdness: the crow was bad and hurting things, she had insisted. But the crow did not try to flee the stones we cast, nor did it try to defend itself. Perhaps its wings were already broken. Or perhaps it was guarding an unseen nest. It fluttered in a harrowing circle on the ground, calling to us, to anyone, for help, while we continued our violent task, until my friend's mother ran out of the house to stop us.

I told Charlie that my problem with a word like "feminine" is that it is a yardstick that measures women's deficiency through its very ambiguity, describing a virtue—or a set of virtues—only in negative. A feminine person is *not* aggressive, *not* brash, *not* sturdy, *not* defensive, *not* punitive, *not* driven, *not* greedy, *not* selfish, *not* self-absorbed, *not*, in fact, anything remotely self-protective or self-advancing. A feminine person must therefore be assumed to be someone who is not only vulnerable and weak, but also sick, if a significant measure of health is one's capacity to set limits that promote one's survival and thriving.

"Your reasoning is straight out of Nietzsche," Charlie said, as if to unsettle me further—he must have understood by then that I was Nietzsche-averse. Still, the softness of his voice felt like a drape intended to protect our intimacy, that warm and formless space between his consciousness and mine: "It's almost verbatim what he says, equating the weak with the sick. Not a pretty part of his thinking, and not one people tend to like, unless they're like me and read him more esoterically. Even your ideas of femininity resemble the ones most people attribute to Nietzsche. And those could easily be viewed as misogynist, don't you think? Vulnerability and softness are *sickness*? Do women have to be masculine to be strong?"

"*Masculine?*"

As though to communicate the scope of his own as yet imperfectly expressed masculinity, he didn't immediately respond to me, only held the delicate wineglass between his fingers and my eyes in his forceful gaze. "Don't the qualities you just listed," he finally said, "qualities you—and Nietzsche, yes—associate with health and that you seem to be privileging . . . aggression, sturdiness, drive . . . Don't they tend to be stereotypes of masculinity?"

I was aware then of wanting something distinctly masculine from him, even as I proceeded to tell him that his entire enterprise of gendering such things was a mistake.

"But you're just as guilty of it," he said, his smile suggestive, defiant. "Your entire enterprise, all your books, seek to define or defend a womanhood that stands in relation to historical and cultural expectations."

When I balked, saying the state of womanhood was quite a different thing from the "virtues" projected upon that state, he paused for so long I assumed he'd assented to my correctness—or given up the chase.

He set down the glass, and I nearly had time to regret vanquishing his last feminizing illusions of me. But with a graver look, he began to speak about a time, several years back, when he and Wah had found themselves at the start of a darkness as terrible as it had become enduring. This was after Wah had met Htet at the convent, he said, when Htet was eleven, and Wah had started trying to facilitate her resettlement. The hope was that they would eventually make Htet their legal adoptee—or Wah's hope, at least. On the one hand, when Wah told him about her encounters with the girl, he was so affected he could hardly breathe. He and

Wah had gone through painful years of infertility, and Htet was in obvious need of what Wah had to give; it seemed to him that to deny either Wah or the girl this chance to love and be loved would be morally reprehensible. Yet he couldn't get past his fear that he might be incapable of accompanying Wah through a shift of orientation by which their lives must necessarily change—must necessarily become centered around someone he'd never met (as in all cases of new parenthood, he was only then absurdly realizing).

A moral philosopher: that was his identity, he said, though none of his research or thinking had prepared him for this, the feeling that he'd completely lost his footing with respect to what was wrong and what was right. Was it selfish to refuse to go along with the plan or noble to spare the girl his doubt and selfishness? While he'd never explicitly rejected the plan to adopt, he'd in effect divorced himself from it by rebuffing every effort Wah made to include him in its enactment. All the paperwork and financial planning, all the video conferences and emailed correspondence with Htet's caretaker and social workers—everything in which his participation was not expressly obligatory, Wah had done without him. And the result was that, already, even then, many months before Htet moved in with them, Wah had come to resent him for his lack of involvement with the girl, just as her relationship with Htet took on a character that he rightly or wrongly began to consider exclusionary. It was as if Wah were assiduously assembling a world in which he saw no honest place for himself.

Grudgingly, he had assented to accompanying Wah to a series of sessions with a couples counselor whom their former contractor (of all people) had recommended. The woman turned out to be something of a contractor herself, if also a clown, with purple streaks in her hair, enormous earrings, colorful patterned outfits, a smiling mouth forever proffering wisecracks, and a single-mindedly constructive approach: for every problem, she promised a practical solution! And as if to prove her wrong, he had found himself behaving unforgivably badly in the sessions, such that one day the woman said, "Let's play a game," and she told Wah to stand on the far side of the room while she herself went to the other side. "Now, when I get too close, say 'stop,'" she instructed Wah. But even when the woman traversed half the room's span, Wah stayed silent. Again, the woman told her, "When I get too close, when I invade your personal space, say 'stop.'" And the woman went back to her side of the room and the same thing happened. And finally, Wah asked, "But what if I don't *perceive* you to be invading my personal space? Do you want me to be honest?" And the woman said, "Yes, of course—when I invade your personal space, say 'stop.'" And just before the woman slammed into her, Wah opened her arms to receive her.

"She looked so lost," Charlie said. "Not Wah. The therapist. As though she didn't know what had happened, if she should cry or feel sorry for Wah or for herself."

He fell silent, and I thought his story was over, that he expected me to infer meaning from it, meaning that would redeem his wife in my eyes; but all I saw, if I may be honest, was one woman playing in a sandbox with hackneyed forms and another too proud or cruel or weak to play along.

"Wah was mocking her," I announced.

"No," Charlie said. He was staring at me now, but I knew it was Wah he was seeing.

"Then she was digging in to prove a point."

"I don't think so."

"Why else," I said, "would she entrench herself in such a defenseless position?"

He watched me with a kind of uncertainty, as though he were split in his loyalties—split between his commitment to the survival instinct we shared, one that left us both defended, and a faith in something as fragile and tenuous as his bond with his inscrutable wife.

"Defenseless . . ." he echoed. "I don't think Wah would conceive of it that way."

I ought to have kept things academic, persisted in our abstract debate all night. But that instinct to destroy the crow shot up in me. The more helpless that crow had become, the worthier of death it had appeared to be.

"That psychologist was a coward," I told him. "I would have said you'd made a suicide pact." And when he didn't respond—he was too stunned, I think, to follow me: "You never wanted children. Wah promised a trap of domesticity . . . She wanted a child, and you promised to make her pay."

There are times when I can't distinguish my habit of honesty from brutality. The look on Charlie's face then was harrowing, broken and shamed. I suppose if I'd been a more "feminine" woman, someone willing to sacrifice her sense of truth for his masculine pride, I would have immediately found a way to recant my diagnosis or to apologize.

"You're right that I make her pay," he said softly. "But I don't mean to. And I don't think she means to treat me as if I'm morally deficient. We've had such a terrible time."

5.

FOR SOME REASON THAT NIGHT—I mean after what I've just described, when I managed to throw open my bedside window to escape the heat without waking Milton—I had the thought that Charlie's reluctance to adopt might be less general than specific, that perhaps it had something to do with Htet's history as a victim of human trafficking. And in my predawn delirium, I imagined that I could see him stalking out past our orchard into the cover of the forest's massed evergreens, as if to evade the same dark forces that had held Htet captive.

But my clear-sightedness was restored, or so it seemed to be, the next morning when, along with an unexpected rain, Eleonore arrived before any of us had risen. As you know by now, my daughter hadn't been in the habit of revealing herself to me, so it was with alarm that I discovered her crouched over a cup of tea at the kitchen table, wearing her father's cast-off camel sweater, her swollen eyes studying me with a look of suffering that did not, for once, immediately communicate blame.

I should tell you that I'd last seen her about a month before, at a panel she'd organized at Columbia, where she was then pursuing her advanced degree and working closely with the Center for Gender and Sexuality Law. The panel, in which she'd invited me to participate along with three other women, was titled "On Justice and Maternity." If I'd vaguely fretted that it had been constructed to serve as a public trial for my maternal failings, and if I'd also feared that I'd inevitably come off as a fraud (as Camus puts it, "Can the man who does not even manage to make justice prevail in his own life preach its virtues to other people?"), I was nonetheless touched that Eleonore wanted to include me. And during the panel discussion—which she cautiously introduced, avowing out of an obligation to honesty, I think, that I was her mother—I was pleased to discover that my fellow panelists were diverse not only in the expected ways, but in their attitudes toward mothering.

One of them, a violinist named Irene, spoke of the ordinary hardship of being a mother today, a hardship that had kept her from realizing even an eighth of what she knew she was capable of accomplishing creatively. And still, she said, now that her twins were in their teens, she was aware of having achieved something elusive, something less tangible than a record of significant performances. "There are performances and there are performances," she said obscurely. "Even something rehearsed in a rush can come off as convincing. But not children. Raising them can't be faked. Their substance has to be nurtured moment by moment, choice by choice. Will I allow myself to snap at them because I haven't been able to rehearse a single phrase without interruption? Will I lock myself in the basement for six hours a day? Should I, instead, master myself enough to teach them self-sufficiency while also considering their reasonable need to be mothered by me?" She said that when she thought about justice in motherhood, she wondered why no one bothered to recognize the important achievement of raising people with substance, people secure enough to know themselves and their values because they had been parented attentively. Speaking for herself, she saw clearly that her greatest achievement had been one she'd done privately: transmitting to her children the best of herself, such that, by some alchemy of grace, they had become "much better than me."

"But we're also not talking about how damaging the idea of equity can be to mothers," said another panelist, an activist named Sonia. Yes, she believed certain men could be better caretakers to their children than women, or as nurturing, as invested . . . But why couldn't we talk about norms within the heterosexual context? Wasn't it true that mothers were more likely to sacrifice for their children than straight fathers, to spread themselves so thin they could barely stand in order to caretake? She herself felt like a victim of the damage done to mothers' rights by gender-neutral custody principles that came out of equal protection doctrine. Yes, she'd made the stupid mistake of signing a prenup when she'd married her attorney husband fifteen years before, an agreement that guaranteed she'd receive neither alimony nor child support if she severed their ties. But he'd been emotionally abusive and resentful of the attention she'd given their infant daughter, not to mention unfaithful. And still, even though she'd been the full-time parent, essentially a *single* parent—whereas he'd worked eighty or ninety hours a week—he'd received 50 percent custody of their sixteen-month-old daughter when they split. "And guess who really paid the price for that 'equity'? Imagine having to hand over your screaming baby every Tuesday to an abusive man you hate, saying goodbye to her for three and a half days, again and again and again. Imagine having to pry her off your arms, telling her—when she's old enough to demand reasons for this barbarism, this total discounting of *her* needs—'The *court* says you have to go to his house, baby; the *court* says *not* going would be breaking the law.' Imagine being in the *brain* of that kid. Imagine how hateful you'd become. Imagine that, by the time you're ten, you trust no one—not the man who takes you away, not the mother who doesn't protect you, not the new wife who thinks he's the angel and you're the demon. Imagine that when you finally begin to act out, he grabs you by the throat and leaves dark bruises that make your teachers call CPS. You'd think *that* would be enough for him to lose his 50 percent, right? Nope. He's the one with money, enough to hire a shark when your mother goes to Legal Aid. And the judge is a man. And the court-ordered psychologist who thinks you're a demon, too, is a man. And what *they're* invested in is the idea that fathers should have the same rights as mothers, despite the gender wage gap, despite their tacit understanding that mothers are prepared to give more of themselves to their children. Which is part of why so many abused women with children don't leave their marriages. They can't afford the fight. And they know that the best way to protect their children is to stay right there in the marriage, right there beside the abuser, in order to protect their children from minute to minute. Battered woman syndrome? Fuck that. More like strong woman syndrome. More like gender equity BS."

"There are other ways to come at all this," said the third panelist, a university staff member named Tina. It was true that she'd always felt mothers were most deserving of her respect because they sacrificed everything for their children. Everything. Yet both of her parents had insisted to her that children are a responsibility for life. In her opinion ("to be honest, and bear with me, I know I'm talking about certain kinds of families"), fathers should be considered the heads of households. Her husband had died when her boys were seven and nine, and only in his extreme absence had she begun to comprehend the extent to which their family was built around the promise of both his care and his strong capacity to protect them. Without that promise, the family unit was not the same; that is to say, the unit was broken, leaving three people even more gravely at risk. Her boys were young men now, and not a day went by that she didn't pray for them to continue to evade jail, the street corner, the morgue. And not a day went by that she didn't pray for them to find the strength to serve as the heads of their own households someday. "Now you see so many women alone in mothering, and just because their men take off, playing with other women or each other like children. And what is that? Is that right? That's not justice. No good comes of it when men don't have a positive place to put their strength. And we have to *want* that for them, *expect* it of them, realize men's strength is also justice for *women*."

"You write about the white maternal experience," said an audience member to me when the floor had been opened for questions. She was standing toward the rear of the hall's raked seats, a quivering microphone pressed to her lips, and after I responded that I begged to differ—that I based my writing very intentionally on my unique experience because I felt incapable of knowing the reality of other people's lives, and because I believed that to pretend otherwise would be to participate in a deceptive flight of fancy—she leaned into the popping mic as if to seek its moral encouragement. (And wouldn't she be right to attempt to refute me? I found myself thinking. Hadn't my entire literary endeavor been built on the premise that I was a kind of everywoman, my experience speaking to an assumed common condition of womanhood, motherhood, wifehood, and, yes, perhaps also of privilege and even whiteness?) "I guess what I'm wanting to say," my interrogator tried, "is that we've just heard about one kind of maternal fear, and I'd like to know how you'd compare it with white maternal anxiety. What do *you* most fear as a mother, I mean besides self-sacrifice?"

"Certainly not my child's death," I replied.

I'd intended to acknowledge the obscene difference between Tina's realities and mine. But as the hall fell into a riveted attention in which I perceived the stirrings of censure, it struck me that my last words could be interpreted as a disparagement of Tina's or as a gesture of disregard for the exigency of my daughter's still-beating heart.

And yet, as I lowered my gaze to Eleonore's, I saw anything but upset in her small and expressive face. She seemed, rather, to be transfixed—by the vision of her death that I'd so cavalierly invoked or by the merciless deficiency of my fear of it.

* * *

It was that same transfixed look I glimpsed in her swollen eyes that morning, when I came down to the kitchen hoping for a swallow of coffee followed by a sprint through the rain—what I'd wanted was to clear my mind, to rinse away any remaining apprehensions about Charlie before the day set in and his departure.

"This is a surprise," I found myself breathlessly telling her from the kitchen doorway.

An almost imperceptible wince passed over Nora's eyes, as if I'd implied that her appearance here was an inconvenience. (And wasn't it? Now there'd be no way to end Charlie's visit with the kind of cozy exchange I'd found so addicting.)

"Sorry for just showing up," she said, and I forced myself to smile into her eyes, trained ambiguously on mine, until she lowered them.

Recently she'd cut her hair, so that it seemed to cradle her skull and convey a will to precision, nothing extraneous and everything just so. And as I stood there taking her in, it occurred to me that the hair had something to do with her body's long habit of thinness, its almost preadolescent intolerance of excess. Other than the aberration of her father's bulky sweater, her outfit, too, emphasized that mastery of exactness: black leggings, pristine sneakers crossed beside the leatherette duffel I'd given her for her last birthday, itself so spotlessly clean it seemed to have been wiped down and trimmed of fraying threads before being packed. She was increasingly like that, Nora, attending meticulously to things while refusing to accumulate them—one pair of flats at a time, one winter coat until it no longer looked presentable—increasingly engaged in a pursuit of control by means of both a radical detachment from materiality and a hypervigilant attention to it. Her only recent concession to beauty or superfluousness was the antique band she wore on her right ring finger, a gift from my late mother that seemed, like the sweater, to have been chosen to put me in my place. And yet here she was, apologizing for assuming a place at home with me.

"Don't be silly," I said. "I'm so happy to see you." I had the thought that I should kiss her, that I wanted to kiss her, but as I went and bent down over the angles of her unsmiling face, I seemed only to be able to offer her my cheek. She smelled of the rain—the damp had brought out the mustiness of the sweater, the floral brightness of her shampooed head—and I wondered what else she'd just come through, why she was here. Had something happened with Yash, the boyfriend whom Milton and I had met a few months previously over an uncomfortably fussy dinner in the city? The boyfriend who—before the salad plates were even cleared—had given me the impression that he wouldn't be staying with her for long, because his ego wouldn't long find her sufficiently flattering.

That was the way it had always been for Nora, a stream of broken attachments and loneliness whose source (at least as identified by those who'd spurned her) was not clumsiness or lack of care on her part, but the same exactitude that manifested in her appearance: a rigor of mind and achievement that had habitually led her to be first in her class, most on top of things, least distracted, least fun to be around, most threatening, and so on. In ninth grade, a ring of girls had surrounded her on a school retreat to enumerate the ways she'd failed to please them, several taking it upon themselves to slap her for the offenses. The next year, when she'd complained to the school authorities about harassment, a teacher had gone on to identify fourteen instances of provocation by a pair of bullies within a single period. "What were they doing?" I'd asked Nora, who, in all her careful self-reliance, had been reluctant to share details with me. "Oh, you know," she'd said. "Laughing about me. Pointing and rolling their eyes. Gossiping. And please don't ask me why, Mom. Why does *anyone* hate me?"

Now she was asking whose car was in the driveway, a question that made me feel somehow embarrassed. And as I made my way to the sink and busied myself with the French press I'd put out the night before in case Charlie rose early, I began to rattle on about my "friend" and his attributes ("Haven't I mentioned Charlie?"), hearing a rising pitch of falseness in my voice. When I allowed myself to glance Nora's way, I saw that she was listening to my string of overstatements and forced enthusiasms with a sort of fixed scrutiny, and for an ugly moment, I felt myself wanting to judge her, too: this was precisely why no one ended up liking her, this somber, dispassionate way she had of taking everything in and assigning it a private value. Shamefully, I wanted to escape, to pretend she'd never shown up and take off running out the patio doors. It was an old feeling, the wish to leave the stifling, difficult atmosphere of home life for the promise of air and space. But when I left Nick, I found I'd only brought that sense of suffocation with me, only missed an opportunity to rescue something breathing and vulnerable, alive.

"I didn't know you had a guest," she said after I'd fallen silent. Any expectancy she'd come into the house with had vanished from her face. And I felt sorry—heartbroken about this ongoing difficulty between us.

"It doesn't matter," I said. "I didn't mean to suggest you shouldn't stay."

"It's all right," she said, motioning to get up. "I'll leave."

There was a squeak on the staircase out in the entryway—not Milton's step. Charlie was coming.

"Please stay," I whispered, more urgently. "He's leaving in a few hours. Meet him—have breakfast with us—then we'll have time."

If I could go back now and change just one thing, it might be that moment. It might be that if Eleonore hadn't been there, looking so unexpected, so radiant with her musty sweater and damp head and suddenly unguarded smile, I would have seen things more clearly.

Or maybe the problem was only ever about how I saw things. Maybe I needed too much to believe in Charlie when he entered the kitchen looking so refreshed and handsome, with his understanding smile taking in everything—the whole scoured picture of Eleonore gazing up at him from the table and me poised by the sink, the rain pattering over the troubled pool outside as though to tell us a story of intimacy and estrangement, oppressiveness and release.

Camus says, "There are places where the mind dies so that a truth which is its very denial may be born." Yet when I remember Charlie then—when I remember all the air and freshness and life-giving hope he brought into that room—I still can't shake my belief in the man he seemed to be.

6.

LOOKING BACK OVER what I have written for you, I fear
I've inadvertently thrown my subject into the background along with Milton, as if against that background
I'd meant to show Charlie and myself in stark relief. I say
inadvertently, and yet isn't that where she always was, Wah—
somewhere off-center, far behind, her innocent head bent by
Milton's in the shadows as they toiled for those of us who
basked in the light? Like a pair of laborers passing their brief
days under some Romantic painting's eternal sky, present
only to give a sense of scale and significance to that actual
subject.

I remember the first time we were together, the four
of us. Several weeks had passed since Charlie had met Eleonore, an encounter that had struck me as both innocent
and reassuring, with the three of us falling into a surprisingly
easy banter under Charlie's influence and then, following

breakfast, with my suggesting that the two of them set off on a walk alone before his flight. Nora's mood had so benefited from his presence, and I must have hoped that their knowing and liking each other better would be good for all of us. (And hadn't that appeared to be the case? "She's such a special person," Charlie had whispered into my ear when they returned from their walk through the drizzle. And Nora, later that night: "I'm embarrassed about how much I told him. He's *so nice*.") I'd hardly communicated with Charlie since; I owed an essay to a magazine, which meant that even Milton was mostly out of my sight line and I'd all but boarded up every entry point to my life. But now the boards were off, the light was streaming in, invitations to speaking engagements had been accepted, and there we were—Milton and I—standing by baggage claim at LAX after our long flight, blinking with fatigue and disorientation as Charlie barged toward us, with Wah trailing behind. It was like we were his whole world, and the world from which he'd come—the world with the wife who happened to be standing by—was the lie.

Well, it would be a lie for me not to admit how unnerved I was by Wah even then. There was the surprise of her girlishly short dress, which struck me as unsophisticated and almost unsuitable for a person of her age. And there was the diminutive, if also disarmingly sincere smile she cast me while I embraced Charlie, pressing one side of my face to his neck. That smile seemed to say, *I see you, Tessa—your attraction to*

my husband, your need to attract, your awareness of the inap-
propriateness of your claims on him, your desire to like me and
hate me and demonstrate your superiority over me, but I will
never permit you to beat me . . .

I imagine some saintlier creature would be above making the kind of spontaneous assessments I'm speaking of,
those imperceptible estimations of power and dominance, by
means of which one determines—sometimes through little
more than a few whiffs in the wind—if another woman will
be a nonplayer in one's life or a friend, a threat or even an
adversary. I swear to you that as I'd stepped off the plane
into Wah's territory, the city in which she had been born
and raised, I'd promised myself that I would find a way to
be her ally. But as the men pulled our bags from the con-
veyor belt, and she and I fumbled through a series of near
wordless exchanges—smiling and nodding, as though we
didn't share the same first language—I found myself unable
to escape the feeling that beneath her sweet, fragile, and, yes,
feminine veneer was a middle-aged woman seething with
something like pride. It could have been the extreme darkness of her eyes, which seemed to rebuff me, or the cant of
her head, angled perpetually down and away from mine, or
the looseness of her long fingers, held against the fabric of
her dress, as though she had no need for the usual forms of
self-protection—of arm crossing or finger pulling—because
she was so very self-satisfied. Even the erratic smiling glances

she cast me as we rolled our bags toward their car seemed to communicate her capacity to see straight through to the worst of me or to the future in which I'd already begun to ruin their lives.

En route to their place, we stopped at my request at Venice Beach, and as we walked along the shoreline toward the misty outline of Santa Monica, we fell into the configuration that would become so natural to us, with me forging ahead, caught up in conversation with Charlie, and Milton and Wah falling farther and farther behind. When I finally looked back to find them, they appeared in the distance down the coast, two tiny figures, a gangling middle-aged man and a reedy, demure woman, bent in intimate conversation and mutual effort against the elements, or perhaps against the shared conditions of their lives.

Milton and I wouldn't speak about that moment until nearly a year later, when he and I were struggling to disassemble the marriage we'd come to see as a sham in its own way. Desperate to understand all that had gone wrong between us, I'd found myself fixating on that first hour with Wah, on the way Milton had fallen in cozy step with her so instantly. Did he remember the walk? I finally asked him. We were at the farm and still living together, though I was packing to relocate to Los Angeles, and I'd come down to the overly warm kitchen to find him boiling pasta and drinking a glass of water at the sink. "Was that when it started," I added, peering into his perspiring face, sunburned and overgrown with resentment, "your disillusionment with me?"

He continued to stare at me with that look of accusation until, suddenly, he chuckled as if at some private joke made at my expense. "I guess that's why I married you," he said. "You put things into words that should never be spoken, make them so completely convincing . . . Yes, I remember the walk. I remember it in *detail*." He turned his head to the bleared view through the window over the sink, a view, I knew, of the pots of tenacious herbs that had been planted by his former wife and that, out of a terrible streak of unhappiness, I'd recently instructed our gardener to allow to die. Or maybe Milton was seeing Wah again as he squinted at the window—some vision of that stoical face confronting the sea changes in her own life. "She talked about serving others, about the call to serve," he said quietly. "How it was her orientation. And I remember thinking, *That's me*. That if I could just soldier on like her, you and I might survive."

Now would probably be the time to address the subject of economics, of how money—or the need of it—can keep a person in a marriage. When I'd wanted to leave Nick, I'd sought counsel from a friend in finance, who helped me determine that Nick and I had just enough to cleave our household into two. When that same friend later introduced me to Milton, one of my first thoughts was that at least there would be the means to end things with him if necessary should we marry. Whereas Charlie and Wah—even then, even together—were barely scraping by. Not that their want of money was immediately apparent to us.

They lived at a sort of midpoint in L.A., close to downtown and the polluting river of the freeway connecting the city's pristine Westside to its eastern realities, on a block of many sprawling houses that over a century ago had attracted the wealthy and now showed all the evidence of its history of white flight, disinvestment, segregation, and poverty, never mind the recent muscle of urban renewal. When we pulled into the neighborhood for the first time after that beach walk, I was unsettled as much by the dissonances on the street as by the ongoing murmur of Wah and Milton trading what sounded like confidences in the back seat—I kept overhearing her mentions of Htet's name and Milton's humming sighs of interest and understanding. Then there was the way that Charlie, from behind the wheel beside me, spoke of the place as though apologizing alternately for its gentrification and diminished state. "That mansion was a brothel for decades," he said, pointing past a tagged freeway overpass to a grand, white-columned revival of some type with delicious wedding-cake moldings. And then, craning his neck the other way, in the direction of a ponytailed blonde jogging purposefully alongside an encampment of tents: "Marvin Gaye lived over there. Shot by his father inside."

At last we parked before their immaculately restored earthy-green Craftsman bungalow, nestled behind a pair of oaks and a sort of woodland native garden. But as we emerged from the car, I was struck less by the property, or its cloaked handsomeness, than by the confounding context in which it was placed. On one side, to the east, stood a Victorian whose rotting eaves, boarded-up windows, and trash-strewn yard made it look as though it had been left to die. And immediately to the west was a scene that could have been straight out of Mayberry, what with an old man rocking on a porch overlooking a well-watered lawn and a pole sporting a weakly fluttering American flag. The man lifted a hand in greeting when Charlie and Wah waved to him.

"That's Ernie," Charlie said, as we began to unload the bags. His tone, or its levity, told me he wanted to tip the scale of our discernment favorably toward the old man, if also away from the unsightliness of the Victorian. "He's been living here since the thirties, except for when he and his parents were relocated to an internment camp during the war." The parents, Charlie explained, had been born in the United States, the mother half German, the father having played pro baseball in Tokyo before marrying. After Japan's defeat, the father had been recruited to translate for the

Americans preparing Tokyo headquarters for MacArthur.
"Of course," Charlie said, "they only kept the house because
the German grandmother was allowed to hold on to it while
they were gone."

"How ugly," Milton responded, no doubt as perplexed
as I by the incongruousness of the old man's personal history
and patriotism.

"Ernie was also a jailer downtown—" Charlie added,
rather cheerily.

"Should we take them to meet him?" Wah asked, though
Charlie was already heading toward the house with our bags.

Camus says, "There is a solitude in poverty, but a solitude
that gives everything back its value." I am thinking of that line
because I grew indistinctly aware of both of those things—
solitude and a dearth of money, if not poverty—over the
course of that first visit with Wah, and I don't want you to
populate the Craftsman, in your mental image of it, with too
many things, too much in the way of cozy collectedness. In
reality, the place was austere to the point of inviting notions
of deprivation. All the necessities—the paint and woodwork
and fixtures—were to perfection, as if what mattered, what
deserved to be tended to, was the aged house, not to mention
the land, both of which had suffered so much for various
reasons through the decades. But the human element? With
the exception of a few evocative pieces, some I've already

mentioned—the banker's lamp, Charlie's great-grandparents' armchairs, an antique brass-frame bed in the guest room, and a secretary desk that Wah had apparently inherited from her father's side of the family—furnishings seemed to have been an afterthought. The whole family slept on mattresses on the floor, if you see my point.

I once mentioned something about this to Wah—I believe I found a way to compliment the sparseness that left a person room to breathe and think—and she looked at me in that disarmingly unguarded way of hers and said something that could have been straight out of the Camus playbook: "I'm embarrassingly dependent on scarcity."

Well, you knew her. I assume you'll agree that when she spoke, it was with few words and often clumsily. She seemed to have an inner confidence, a well of things she wanted to bring out in speech, and an outward diffidence. I didn't ask her to elaborate on what she'd meant by that—"dependent on scarcity." I probably chalked it up to things I'd read about her online, that she'd come from a childhood of relative poverty and upheaval in L.A., that she'd lost her refugee mother when she was nine . . . The most obvious explanation for her preference for barrenness was the dispossession of her past.

But for all that, I began to sense—even during that first visit—that her aversion to material plenty was tied in some way to her willingness to suffer the disappointments of her marriage to Charlie. She was so alone so much of the time, alone with Htet, alone in the scrappy effort to bridge the divide between their incomes and the demands of raising a child in L.A. It's not that I knew anything about the extent of that aloneness yet, though I began to comprehend it—even to perceive something about how the aloneness, when coupled with the economic struggles she faced, enhanced what she had in abundance: the strength of her bond with Htet, her pleasure in the same house that Charlie wanted so much to escape.

That first evening at the Craftsman, before dinner and dusk had set in, she invited me to join her for a drink in the back garden. As I've tried to suggest, the house was modest in the scheme of things, yet the backyard was one of the most distinctive I've seen anywhere, with an original barn where a horse and carriage must have been kept, and a fountain that could have come straight out of an old mission, and a vine-covered arbor where—save for the drone of incoming planes chasing the exhaust over the nearby freeway—it was pleasant to sit and survey the beds of succulents and flowering natives, and also the trees that seemed to want to shield us from the apprehensions of the neighborhood and the world at large.

She was like that, Wah, capable of creating an ambience that nearly convinced you that disharmony and degradation didn't exist. There had apparently been a basketball court in the rear when they'd moved in, and she'd persuaded some obliging neighbor to help her jackhammer it into plate-sized pieces that she'd used to form the garden's raised borders and dry arroyos and winding paths laced with creeping thyme. It was all as pleasing as the indoor vintage touches, the tiles and pendant lights, and those plumbing fixtures that she'd apparently dredged up from the pits of some freeway-underpass salvage yard. Sitting with her on that first evening, in the shadow of the barn's converted hayloft where Charlie kept his home office and was presently entertaining Milton, I nearly found myself believing that, in spite of Charlie's accounts of their marital hardships, Wah had found a way to pull it off: a perfect domestic life.

But, of course, all I had to do was turn my eyes next door to see the upper stories of the Victorian, which from the backside appeared even more decrepit and deserted than from the street. All I had to do was open my ears to hear the hum of the highway or glance upward to spy the underbelly of some encroaching commercial plane bent on buzzing the houses in the economically bipolar community. Unpacking with Milton in the guest room earlier, I'd peered through a window to glimpse a grown man swerving wildly on a bicycle down the street, as if toying with a wish to smash each luxury vehicle he passed. Then there was Htet, who hadn't made an appearance in the hours since our arrival and whose absence, strikingly, neither Charlie nor Wah had remarked on. "She's been caught up with some boy," Milton had whispered when we were stretched out on the guest room bed for a few moments. "Supposedly goes missing for hours. It's more of a friendship than anything. Not a problem when Charlie's away, but he's very sensitive about it." Sensitive enough not to have mentioned anything about this boy—or even much about Htet—to me.

In the garden with Wah, avoiding the sight of her profile in the darkening arbor, I began to be aware of music, an old swing tune drifting toward us from Ernie's side of the cedar fence dividing the two properties. That music, reassuring and warm, seemed to want to instruct me to be calm, to hold a more charitable view of the woman next to me. And yet, when I glanced quickly at Wah—at her mild expression as she stared out toward the fountain and Ernie's property—it struck me that she was someone who wasn't easy to like.

Having written that last line, I realize that I said something similar about Nora to you (something that could easily be said about me). And it's true that Nora and Wah shared a certain inaccessibility that could be described alternately as mysterious and off-putting. Like Nora, Wah gave little access to what was under the hood, and, like Nora, she appeared delicate. But Wah's delicacy was just the opposite of Nora's ironclad, willed one; it seemed to be all about relinquishing, all about deference. I had the impression, sitting there, that I could crush her if I so much as reached out too quickly— that it wasn't right for a woman to be so fragile.

"Isn't it lovely?" Wah said. It took me a moment to understand that she was referring to the sound of Ella Fitzgerald's voice, now drifting over the fence. "Ernie plays songs from the forties while making dinner, sits on his porch drinking wine in the afternoon. Every day I'm reminded what a privilege it is to live beside him." How lonely she sounded, as though she were speaking of her isolation on the block. Or with Charlie.

"You've created something beautiful here," I said, perhaps to assuage my guilt about that isolation, for hadn't I cultivated Charlie's interest in me?

"It doesn't matter," she replied.

She was always surprising me. I asked what she meant by that, and she turned her gaze in my direction with such openness I felt myself flushing.

"I should have written another book," she said. "Charlie's hard on me about it."

"Is he?"

She laughed with something like pain in her eyes, and I wondered if she feared Charlie had complained about her to me.

"We need the domestic more than books," I argued, though immediately Camus's Don Juanian refrain about the passionate mother or wife came to mind, how her heart is closed to the world. And hearing the disingenuousness in my voice, I went on: "What is the world at large without every smaller, domestic one? I hate men for making us feel that the domestic is meager. It's everything."

Wah's searching gaze, trained now on mine, seemed to be on the lookout for discord between my proclamations and unvoiced meanings. I kept telling myself to smile, to nod, but the uncharitable part of me held out, held her in contempt for allowing Charlie to succumb to his escape fantasies while she squandered herself on this little household endeavor—one that had been built on a foundation of marital trouble, if Charlie was to be believed. I don't remember where Camus says we *can't* give ourselves completely or else we can't create, but that just about captures the gist of the feminine tragedy, or at least why Wah hadn't flourished as a writer, as I saw it.

"I guess I do have a book I've been trying for," she said, still squinting into my eyes. "I don't know if it's this way with you, but sometimes I wonder when I'll get to write what I want to write."

"What you *want* to write?" I really had no idea what she meant.

"Living here," she said, her eyes traversing the flowers and trees, "it's difficult to ignore the ghosts, the people who've tried to make this home, somewhere safe and nice."

I asked her to whom she was referring, and it was odd how fluent she became. She said that when Ernie and his Japanese-German parents had moved to the block back in

'38, racial covenants had still been in effect. The woman who'd built her own house had been the chapter president of the Daughters of the Confederacy, though by '48, when the covenants were struck down, she and most of the others who'd settled the block had been scared off. For those who remained and came in, it really could have been something. But the freeway came through in the '60s, and whole blocks were taken out, beautiful squares, along with every last illusion that segregation was a thing of the past. So much unleashed over these streets—dust from leaded gasoline, drugs, bullets, roving men—three brothels on this block, at least. Now it was tire dust, particulates, jet fuel. No one wanted to admit that the incoming planes had been rerouted over the poorest parts of L.A. As if the freeway pollution weren't enough. As if this community needed noise pollution and more toxins. "You see too many children in wheelchairs around here," she said. "Sometimes I get so overcome, so upset by the injustice. Then I speak with Ernie. He can't hear the jets because of his age." She laughed, and for an instant my hope that we might be friends returned. But she said, too sentimentally for my taste, "It's not that things don't upset Ernie, only that he's seen so much. He carries all this past inside him."

"You don't have to write it, you know," I told her. "Whatever book it is you're 'trying for'—about Ernie? The street?" In truth, I found the idea of such a book to be appalling. It was enough that Wah was a gentrifier; now she was going to appropriate the neighborhood's history of segregation and white flight? I think I probably wanted to avert her from disaster with some cliché like, *Stay in your lane*. Instead I said, "You don't have to sentence yourself to duty."

For a moment, she turned her attention to me, and I was surprised by the way some of the girlishness had drained from her face, so that she looked all at once tired, sallow. I found myself looking away, to the dimming view of her succulent garden, but its spines and blooms appeared speckled with fine black soot now, something I attributed to my imagination and the hulking ugliness of the Victorian beyond the cacti.

"That's a sad case," she said, noticing the direction of my gaze.

She began to tell me of the woman who'd lived in the Victorian for decades, beginning in the '70s—a single mother and hoarder who'd been reluctant to leave. "Ernie says she thought terrible things would happen if she moved out, that by staying here she was holding everything together, the block, her property. When the son finally persuaded her to relocate to a convalescent home, everything—walls and walls of her belongings—stayed where they'd been, frozen in time. Even the trash she'd set out on the porch on her way out stayed there for years. Like a fairy-tale symbol of something."

"Of the downside"—I'd wanted to say *evils*—"of gentrification."

"Of the dangers of being a woman alone," she said, with a meaningful glance at me. "Of being a mother alone, left with your duty."

7.

I CAN STILL PICTURE THE WAY Htet came sauntering into the dining room that first night. Wah had set out an array of noodle salads, thickly sauced vegetables, and fried chicken—the last being Charlie's attempt to replicate the flavors from a Kuala Lumpur KFC where Htet had often gone to hawk her traffickers' wares (and to swipe the odd drumstick, her favorite, from customers too stingy to offer her the equivalent of a quarter). Instead of acknowledging us, the girl walked skeptically up to the platter that Charlie had moved across from me, where he wanted her to sit.

"Htet," he prodded her. "Say hello to Tessa and Milton."

I should mention that she had come in wearing a backward-facing baseball cap over her wild mane of hair and a crop top exposing her slim waist and iron belly button ring. What with that and the enormous hoop earrings framing her darkly made-up face, she seemed to be flirting unselfconsciously with clichés of youth, seduction, and alt culture at the same time, daring any of us within range to stare at her or get the hell out of her life. Still, when we all sat and she finally glanced at me, it was with an interest and even a sweetness that took me by surprise.

"Why don't you pass the chicken to Tessa," Wah suggested to her.

Htet served herself a generous portion before shoving the platter my way, and for a while I did my best to match the pace of her eating, washing down each oily bite with mouthfuls of the wine that Charlie kept refilling for me. It was poignant to see her enjoying her food; it made me wonder how often she'd had to steal to feed herself in Kuala Lumpur. And I was moved by the way Wah took such vigilant measure of her over the course of the meal, as if she had to cram what should have been a whole run of mothering Htet, from infancy to adolescence, into every moment they had left together under this roof—all the attentiveness, all the encouragement, all the gnawing concern and protectiveness and belief.

"Do you have a baby?" the girl suddenly asked me, in an English that had a thuggish quality, a Brooklyn toughness that could have been imported from some procedural she'd watched on TV.

"A baby!" I said with a laugh that I regretted as soon as I noticed Wah's serious expression.

"We have three children," Milton put in, wiping the grease from his mouth. "Two sons. They're grown now. And a daughter."

"Charlie didn't say that," Htet told him. "Show me her picture."

I expected one of her parents to remind her of something like discretion, but they just looked on in their separate ways while Milton pulled out his phone and began swiping through it until he landed on an old shot of Nora, from when her hair had been long and she'd carried more weight and color in her cheeks. It wasn't a flattering picture outwardly, but it nevertheless flattered *her*, for if a photo is a thermometer of sorts, giving a reading of a person's inner well-being, then the one Milton held up toward Htet's circumspect eyes made Nora out to be better off than she'd been for a very long time.

"Looks like Tessa, don't you think?" Milton asked the girl.

"She looks like her father," I interjected.

Milton appeared as bewildered as I was by my denial of Nora's obvious resemblance to me.

"You're not the father?" Htet asked him.

"*Htet*," Charlie said.

"It's okay to *ask* things," she shot back before turning to Wah. "Right, Amay?"

"How about you help me with the dishes," Wah answered with a penetrating smile. She pushed herself up from the table and began to pick up our plates, though Htet didn't make a move to help her yet.

I think it was then that I began to comprehend the isolation Charlie had complained of, to conceive of him not just as a would-be escapee from domestic life but as someone who was being discounted. He seemed so apart from his family. It wasn't only the way the girl had challenged him, or the exhausted, mildly hostile look now spreading across his face, a look that reminded me of how he'd appeared in the rear of Milton's car en route back from that dinner with my editor in the city. It was the current of loyalty that ran from the mother to the daughter and back, an understanding that excluded him, left him feckless.

"Tell Tessa and Milton about your new school, Htet," he tried.

"I don't like it!" she announced.

Charlie ignored this and began explaining that it was a charter school for girls. "Htet is lucky to attend it. The place where she was before . . . they didn't appreciate her talkativeness in class."

"Not in *class*, Charlie," she corrected him. "On the field." She turned to me now with a kind of daring. "If someone gives me shit, I don't take it."

"The dishes, Htet," Wah said, and I noticed Charlie shake his head at her, or was it at the girl?

Htet disregarded them. "Someone always gets shit," she kept telling me. "At this new place, they say every girl has a voice. A lie. They only like girls who talk. A lot, a lot. Talk all the time about what they think, what they have. And the girls only respect if you have what they have. You have more of something, you're shit. Less of something, you're shit. I got attitude, so I'm okay. But some girls, they *like* to be quiet. So they're shit."

I admit to being won over by her "attitude," yet something about Wah's own quietness over that mounting stack of dishes at her end of the table prompted me to argue, "Isn't it a good thing for quiet girls to be encouraged to speak up? To *assert* themselves? Raise their *voices*."

Htet stared at me for a moment. She was still holding her fork, and I had the panicked thought that she might fling it at my face, but she dropped it with a clatter and thrust herself back from the table. "Sorry, Amay," she said, picking up her plate. "I can help." And then, almost quietly: "Some people already have too much voice."

Whenever I crossed paths with the girl during the remainder of that visit, and, in fact, during all the subsequent ones save for the last, she was polite enough, acknowledging me with a nod or a brief greeting, though never again making an effort to engage with me. There was just one time, other than during

81

our final encounter, when I saw her with the boy—that friend whom Charlie had apparently been so worried about and whose name, as I would learn, was Joaquin.

It must have been two or three visits in. Milton and I had been off with Charlie in Topanga for a hike, and when we returned in the smudged light of late afternoon, there they were, the two of them, sitting on the curb before the Victorian. Not that I spotted them straightaway. It was deceptive, how everything could appear peaceful in their neighborhood, handsome and reassuring, as if you'd left the city's chaos to find yourself in some better sector. I recall looking out my passenger window, as we pulled up, at a small swirl of fallen leaves skirting the edges of Ernie's lawn, and then glancing over to find the old man staring back at me from the rocking chair on his porch. I nearly waved, but we hadn't been introduced, and I suddenly became aware of Charlie's apprehension behind the wheel as he glared through the windshield at the two teenagers, poised about twenty feet beyond the canopy of the Craftsman's oaks.

"That asshole," he murmured, turning off the ignition.

They were both wearing shorts, Htet and Joaquin, their limbs gleaming in the shade, though that was as far as any resemblance between them went. He was so much bigger, older looking in his rumpled T-shirt, his face soft and round. Still, she appeared tougher than he did, with those giant earrings like amulets defending her chiseled features, and all that hair spreading out from beneath her cap, and something guarded about the way she sat, hunched over her spread knees. Joaquin had been smoking a cigarette, and seeing Charlie's car, he moved to extinguish the thing, but Htet grabbed it from between his fingers and put it between her lips, as if to tell Charlie—all of us—to fuck off.

"Everything all right?" Milton said from the rear.

That seemed to be all Charlie needed. He threw open his door, and out we went, into the family bitterness that I still don't fully understand.

Htet didn't back down as we approached, just kept staring at us and blowing smoke in our direction, while the young man lowered his eyes to the asphalt as if in preparation for a scolding.

"Please take our guests inside, Htet," Charlie told her when we drew near.

"Not my guests," she said. And then she looked up at me. "No offense."

"None taken," I said.

"I asked you not to smoke around here," Charlie told the young man, who tilted his coppery eyes up at us as if to begin to apologize.

"You ask him not to smoke *in there*," Htet countered, tipping her head toward the Victorian.

"Let me be clearer, then," Charlie said in a voice unsteady with anger. He could be such an imposing and authoritative man, only for the uncertain boy in him to dissolve that man to pieces. "No smoking, *period*." He pointed a territorial finger at Htet. "Not near *her*. Not near my house. Not in *there*." That same finger turned accusatorially to the Victorian. "No going in there *ever*. Not unless you want me to call the cops. Or Duane."

I thought I had misheard—no one had mentioned a Duane to me—though Joaquin's face suggested he'd understood every detail of Charlie's warning. His mouth pursed, and he nudged Htet as if to ask her in the gentlest way possible if she could let this go, the cigarette, this fight.

But she glared up at Charlie. "You don't care he has nowhere to sleep?"

"Charlie?" came Wah's voice. A gust of wind rose as I turned to see that she had emerged from her house and was standing on the Craftsman's broken concrete walkway. She held down the skirt of her gauzy Indian-print dress and cupped her eyes, as though to spare herself an onslaught of wind-blown contaminants while squinting out at us. "You've met Joaquin!" she called uneasily—I guess to Milton and me.

As she began to move toward us down the path, Htet put out the cigarette, toeing it on the asphalt with the tip of her boot, and the young man straightened himself up with an expression of respect laced with dread.

"Htet," Wah said, joining our group, "did you introduce Tessa and Milton to our friend?" It was so subtle, the way she turned her back slightly on Charlie, distinguishing herself from him while also interceding on his behalf with the young man.

"They don't want to be introduced," Htet answered bitterly.

"I do!" Milton chimed in.

Wah was the only one to laugh at that. "Meet our friends Tessa and Milton," she said to Joaquin, offering him a smile that appeared to come from some private source, the same calm and comprehending one she tapped when communicating with Htet. "They'll be staying another night here—maybe you've seen them around before?"

Joaquin hesitated, his gaze latched to hers, but finally he nodded our way, his eyes flicking up to mine so that I saw, in their proud depths, I don't know . . . a question. Or maybe I was only asking myself why I, a relative stranger to this family, was being welcomed into their house while he was being denied access to the empty hovel next door.

It was too much. I looked away to Charlie, whose expression spoke of frustration and, above all, shame: he couldn't stand being managed by his wife. Emasculated, I guess he would say. Charlie, who wanted to roam from the female-dominated home that was his, from the expectations and comforts that had become liabilities in his eyes, though they were the very things a boy like Joaquin might have longed for. Is it wrong to belittle one man's suffering because another's seems so much harsher, so much more concrete?

"I'm so sorry about all this," I heard Wah say, and when I looked back at her smiling face, I saw that she was apologizing to Joaquin for Charlie's meanness and probably also to the rest of us for the spectacle of their domestic drama.

"You don't need to do that," Charlie told her sharply. "You don't need to apologize for my behavior."

Milton put a protective hand on my back. "Now, now," he murmured, words that Charlie didn't seem to hear and that Wah could have assumed were meant for her.

For a moment, she froze with that smile, her eyes glassy. Then she began to laugh again, reminding me of a Stepford wife stupidly amused by the antics of cantankerous men. She reached out to gently take hold of Charlie's bare arm—he was wearing an old tennis shirt—and he visibly bristled at her touch, so that suddenly all his nervous, jittery tendencies in the dark made sense to me. He was forever waiting to be attacked, I realized, to be struck, and also to strike back. But why? Who knows what the sources of another's sensitivities are? Another's heart, as I see it, is uncharted territory.

Wah started heading back up the path, pulling Charlie along and calling to Htet over her shoulder—something about how the girl should come inside to get some snacks and water for Joaquin—while Milton and I dumbly followed after them.

I'd forgotten about Ernie, and when I glanced in the direction of his porch, I found the old man observing us with an unnerving expression, neither warm nor unkind. I wonder if he sensed anything as he watched us from that fixed vantage point. If he could have believed that within the year, out of everyone before him, only I would be left here.

8.

Y OU'D THINK THAT his shameful display of ill will toward
Joaquin would have made me lose my respect for
Charlie. Or that my continued interest in him could only be
explained by something as reckless as lust. But it was never
as simple as anything like that with him. Before Charlie, I'd
been certain of so much, yet my certainty had backed me
into a corner, kept me on a Sisyphean mountain of moral
outrage, if you like, smugly trudging up the landscape of our
times and slipping back down whenever I encountered the
limits of my perspective, of my heart. Even my ambivalence
about Charlie seemed like a path off that mountain of conviction, as though for me he were some skewed version of
what the goddess Nemesis once represented for Camus. You
see, much as Sisyphus stood for Camus as the figurehead
for his early phase, Nemesis represented what he hoped to
achieve ultimately with his work. In ancient Greek religion,

she was the goddess of retribution, ruthlessly punishing those who exceeded limits; and for Camus—because she represented the moderation that accounted for the variety of human experience and perspectives—she was also the goddess of love.

On the evening after our encounter with Htet and Joaquin, we adults were joined for dinner at the Craftsman by a pair of Charlie's friends, a charming young man and his distinguished historian husband, both wonderful raconteurs whose verbal excitements were frustrated by the way Wah kept fluttering up from the table to cart off dishes or top off glasses or ply us with platters so artfully displayed I felt almost punished by them, as if these additional fruits of her labor were meant not so much to give us pleasure as to emphasize her sacrifice. I didn't consciously arrive at the idea then, but something about her that night reminded me of my mother, who had been a perfect hostess and had habitually made me feel that her life was being spoiled by the bottomlessness of my needs.

"Seriously," I found myself declaiming to the table, after a reenactment of the moment I'd denied fearing Nora's death at that panel on motherhood and justice, "wouldn't it be almost *immoral* to worry that your fortunate daughter might prematurely die—or, for that matter, to grieve too much if that did happen? Children all over the world are dying in poverty every day, and do we spend every day fretting about how to prevent that or grieving them? Just think of the kid next door. Joaquin."

With that, I threw a pointed look at Charlie, daring him to explain the boy's situation to us, not to mention the dubious morality of his treatment of him. I felt Charlie rise to the challenge: he peered at me, his face flushing, so that I sensed that whatever he came out with next would ignite a debate. How often I allowed people to stand for concepts in those days, as Charlie would soon point out to me.

Suddenly Wah stood from the table, an anxious look on her face. "If something were to happen to Htet," she said, "I'd . . ." For a moment, she seemed too overcome to continue. Then she said, "I'd see it as my responsibility to grieve."

When no one made a move to respond—no one save for the historian's husband, who pushed up the frame of his glasses as if to force some sympathetic comment from his head—she began swiftly encircling the table, picking up our dirty plates, her default practice, with a smile that I interpreted as at once hurt, proud, and conciliatory. She could never simply agree with me, Wah. She always had to push back with some idea that threw a moral shadow onto mine—and then retreat, like a victim of my cat swipes, when *she* could have been called a cat, that misogynist cliché. Soon she was reliably sulking off to the kitchen with all those dishes, telling us she would return when dessert and coffee were ready.

"We found out they won't be making a film of her book," Charlie announced, following her with his eyes.

He'd never mentioned the possibility of a film to us, and when Milton asked for details, Charlie proceeded to explain that Wah's book had been optioned after its publication by a producer, who'd called yesterday to say he'd lost his nerve, or rather was "shelving the project" for the time being.

"And you know why?" Charlie went on, giving me a sidelong look. Because they needed someone of Southeast Asian descent to direct, he continued, preferably a woman. But no one knew of such a person with sufficient clout *and* interest. And who would play Wah? An Anglo-Korean? An Anglo-Chinese? Wouldn't that be a tad wrong? And Htet? It was hard to imagine they'd be able to find a Muslim-Burmese child actor. Not that anyone knew Htet's precise ethnicity— she'd been yanked away from her mother and brother at such a young age that all she could recall were broken bits of family lore that placed her biological father in the military. In other words, Charlie kept on, for this producer the most important thing was to find actors whose racial profiles matched Wah's and Htet's—or Htet's assumed one. Forget about talent, inspiration, a soulful match. Forget about an artist's capacity for empathy, imaginative leaps . . .

Any playfulness had fled from Charlie's eyes, leaving the unwieldy look of a man possessed, a man threatened to be overtaken by notions with which his world no longer concurred. It frightened me, and I had the protective thought that he wasn't the one to be toying with such notions. That to see him doing so was indecent, something that explained the way the historian had begun to wipe his pale forehead with the napkin he kept refolding, while Milton fondled the stem of his wineglass as though he were considering snapping it. Only the younger man gazed with relative interest at our host, his warm eyes searching now past the frame of his glasses for some line to catch amid Charlie's tossed out unorthodoxies, some way to stay with him or to reel him in.

"Listen," Charlie continued, as if *he* were the one bent on saving us. "Of course people should have the chance to tell their own stories whenever possible. But what about stories of the *truly* marginalized? People who don't fall into well-established categories, or who are so disenfranchised they have no access to literary and filmmaking systems?" He knew a screenwriter, a friend of a friend, who'd spent years living in Hawaii. She'd written a pilot for a series with a multiracial lead, a woman who was part Native, part Portuguese, part Japanese, or something. Now the pilot was being made, and the producers couldn't find an actress famous enough to carry the series with the same ethnic mix. So what did they do? Cast someone less famous? Cast an actor of another multiethnic makeup, someone who could pass? No. They changed the plot and cast a white lead.

"That's one story, Charlie," I interrupted. "It would be extreme to extrapolate from it."

"Why do you use that word, 'story,'" he said, "to discredit certain experiences?"

From the kitchen, I heard a door shut. It occurred to me that Wah might have been bothered by our discussion of such subjects in her absence, that she could have gone out for some air. But Charlie hadn't seemed to hear: he kept looking at me with those riveted eyes, baiting me to respond.

"What about your friend?" I said, giving in. "Your screenwriter friend who lived in Hawaii. Is she even multiracial herself?"

"That's not the point," he said.

"Then what *is* the point?" Milton asked. He wasn't being insolent, though I heard an undertone of hardness in his voice. Only when Milton drinks does the soft blanket of his tolerance begin to fall away.

"Yes," the historian chimed in. "What *is* your point? Are you suggesting we should recolonize narratives that aren't ours? Revert to displays of *Orientalism*—"

"My *point*," Charlie said, "is that we've lost our sense of *connectedness*." His eyes jerked back to the shuttered window, beyond which I knew the Victorian stood. "My *point* is that we're heading dangerously toward a kind of segregationism in the name of morality. Take Htet's school fundraiser last week. They wanted to be more inclusive. Great. Instead of targeting wealthier families as usual, they invited everyone. Wonderful, right? But what they do is group parents by zip code—by 'neighborhood,' excuse me. So you come to a dinner strictly with others in your 'community.' Well intentioned? Maybe. Probably. But we might as well bring back the old racial covenants. Don't laugh. I know you're trying to goad me, Tessa, but this is *real*. This is them not trusting rich folks to treat lower-income ones with respect. Not trusting folks from around here to respect *themselves* enough not to be harmed by rubbing elbows with the wealthy. Everyone wants *lines*. We want them because it feels too hard to deal with each other as *humans*."

What I wanted was for him to stop. *I* wanted a line— wanted to draw one, in front of everyone present, between his argument and me, between the safety of our private, nocturnal debates and the perils of this public performance. But I seemed to have lost the intellectual route out of this exposed, unsafe place.

"Get some control of yourself, Charlie," I said. I wanted to tell him, *Shut up, for God's sake, or everyone here will think you're reactionary*. "You're going too far in your argument. It's *excessive*. By your reasoning, we might as well give up on inclusivity altogether—"

"What are you talking about?" he cried.

"What I'm talking about is if you don't watch out some- one is going to come and lop off your head!"

I thought that was it: semi-affectionate hand slap delivered and the whole unpleasant business done with. But a flood of emotion rose in Charlie's eyes, and I was suddenly afraid he would do something as injudicious as start to weep.

"If I'm guilty of extremes, Tessa, so are you," he assured me. "Forgive me for this, but when you question the morality of mourning for your own child because children the world over are unjustly dying, you're dehumanizing everyone. Making Nora and Joaquin and the world's suffering children into abstractions, stereotypes."

I began to protest—he was being absurd, unfair!—but he raised a cautionary hand and told me, "Let me finish," so that I fell silent. And then he said, his tormented eyes chastening me, "You can't seem to believe in your ability to understand people with different circumstances, to really feel for them. To *feel* for someone like Joaquin. So it forces you to deny yourself the experience of feeling for your own 'fortunate' child. That's the most tragic thing I've ever heard you say. And it doesn't do this world, or its children, or Nora, *or* Joaquin, any good. It would be better to get down on your knees and beat your chest and tear out your hair and sob for all of them."

9.

I HAVEN'T TOLD YOU YET about what really ended things with Nick, the specific night that led me to confront the reality that I could never be what he needed. I just used the phrase "confront the reality," but what is reality but our perception of it? What is falling out of love but a sort of crisis of perception? I was so wedded back then to the idea that reality could be cleaved from make-believe, but perception is such a malleable thing, both real and make-believe. If today I see Charlie's old wingback chairs in this living room as manifestations of his regard for history, those chairs will look like treasures instead of junk. If I see Charlie himself as decent and brilliant in spite of everything he's done, those qualities remain part of the reality of who he is to me. If back then I could have seen myself as some semblance of what Nick needed me to be, surely our story would have ended differently.

I remember how irritable I was on that night with Nick. Eleonore was ten and in fifth grade, and maybe because I tended to be so absorbed with my writing—or because group activities always left her feeling pained—she had an urgent need for me to volunteer at her school regularly. As you might imagine, the role of parent volunteer wasn't quite natural to me. That day I'd spent several hours manning a snack table on a hot patch of pavement, swinging between feelings of resentment and judgment and envy. None of the other mothers present seemed to be conflicted about having given up hours of their day; in suits or jeans or summer dresses, they dashed around refilling platters and organizing children into lines, as if to proclaim, *We got this!* Or, no: *We love this!* But that wasn't quite it, either. *We are this!* Yes. *We are this!* "This" being the amalgamation of types, roles, and ideals they appeared almost effortlessly to embody: graceful homemaker, ass-kicking professional, tireless child advocate. In other words, the contemporary feminine icon of success, poised down to her manicured fingers, never a gray hair showing, plucked, fit, content to manage logistics in the kitchen or the boardroom—or the bedroom, presumably. One has to wonder if the extent to which women willingly play various roles (such that the roles themselves appear to define them) is not itself a powerful example of perspective bending. How else do so many of them succeed at overlooking the fundamental injustice of having to do and be just about everything? Men get to act; women, to playact or risk ruin.

Well, the entire performance of maternal involvement was on my mind as I put Nora to bed that night. It is difficult for me under certain conditions, even now, to really look at Nora—I mean to sit with her and be still and simply take her in. I think a part of that difficulty, a superficial part, has to do with how much she can, in fact, resemble Nick. It's something in the cheekbones and the set of the eyes in her head, something about the line that runs from the center of her nose down to the lips. That line is just askew, a subtle crookedness accentuated when she smiles or smirks. I remember, that night, waiting at the foot of her bed as she propped a stuffed animal on her nightstand and then fiddled with her retainer. She was a bit plump back then—adorable, really—and prone to leaving everything she'd gotten into during the day on her bedroom floor. And as I asked her if she'd eaten anything after brushing her teeth and told her that she would need to be better about cleaning her room the next day, I was aware of not quite being able to look at her face, of something fiercer than agitation overcoming me.

I rarely lost my temper, but to gird myself against that possibility—and perhaps to avoid further engaging with her and extending the whole bedtime routine—I began to fixate on the drink I would have as soon as I'd managed to extricate myself from her room. Sherry. Sherry, yes. But why sherry? I could never admit to myself how much like my mother I had become. I kissed Nora and switched off her light and, in a cabinet off the kitchen, found the bottle of scented oloroso sherry I'd stashed behind the other alcohols that Nick liked. Only when I'd drained the first little glass of the mahogany liquid did that feeling of unstoppable upset return. Nick had left a pile of encrusted dinner dishes and pots in the sink; in fairness to him, he'd cooked that night, and the understanding between us was that on such occasions, which were not infrequent, I would do the tidying. But as I filled myself another glass, I couldn't seem to get going on cleaning. Nick liked the kitchen to be immaculate, and I did, too. And yet it was mostly for show. Mostly to suggest to ourselves, if not to the world, that we were grown up, responsible, presentable, living in harmony. Staring at those dirty dishes, I seemed to see how far I'd gone astray. I'd wanted my life to be about reflection, close attention, an artful shaping of insight, but the artifice of our domestic success left little room for so much as an uninterrupted thought. Why should Nick, who was no longer vocationally driven and who never put Nora to bed, be reading in the living room while I scoured pans and wiped away saucy fingerprints?

I must have drained the second glass by the time I looked up from those dishes to see Nick standing in the kitchen doorway with a particularly crooked line running from his nose to his bared teeth. Or perhaps it would be more accurate to say: to his bared contempt for me. Yet I'm doing him a disservice, reducing his expression to one of contempt, for his face also shone with guilt, as though he were about to fail me by broaching a subject that would be painful for both of us.

"What did I do?" I found myself sputtering.

A flash of surprise lit up his face, and for a moment I thought he would laugh or find some other way to rescue us from the undeniability of whatever it was he was now perceiving. But he said, with a sadness in his searching eyes, "I was in the hallway when you put Nora to bed. I heard you talking. It's not healthy, how you are. Burdened. Like you don't want to be there. It's not good for her."

It was as near as Nick would come to an insurrection. I had married him, I suppose, for his mildness, for the sense of safety I felt with him. But that safety, if not the mildness, had its limits.

"Why don't you put her to bed, then?"

"Come on, Tess."

Looking into those tired, suffering eyes, I felt as if the entirety of my maternal situation had been a setup for just this: this relentless feeling of insufficiency. Of course, he was right; but he was also off the hook—off the hook because Nora's greater need for me (due to nature or social programming or only that legacy of maternal aloofness that ran like

101

its own crooked line through my family) left him largely out
of its calculus of responsibility.

"What she needs," he said—as if it didn't occur to him
that I, too, had needs—"what *I* need, is a feeling that we
matter. To you, Tessa. That we matter to you more than
anything. Do we?"

All I had to do was reach out and meet him, walk
through the door of his longing. But the sherry bit at the
back of my throat, and I couldn't speak.

Even when he said, "If you had to choose between us
and your writing, would it even be a choice?"

It wasn't so much a choice as a reflex when, on a cold November morning, I hung up the phone with my agent and immediately dialed Charlie. About a month had passed since our
dinner with the historian and his husband, a month of relative silence between us, because I was having such a hard
time forgiving him for his diatribe about my insufficiency
of heart, so to speak.

Now he answered in a voice thick with sleep and disorientation. I'd forgotten the time difference, and the strangeness
of hearing him like that, of hearing his intimate voice, reserved
for someone with whom he shared a home or a bed, made all
the strangeness of our recent distance return to me.

"Let me call back at a better time," I stammered.

"No," he said. "What is it? Tell me."

I blurted out the news, even as it began to dawn on me that I hadn't yet told Milton about the prize, that Wah might be in bed beside Charlie, straining to hear every word I said.

"Oh, Tessa . . . Tessa," he kept saying. He could have been telling me he loved me.

"Let me buy you a plane ticket," I blurted out. "Come to the ceremony." And then, to cover my embarrassment about having so obviously laid claims to him, "I know Milton and Nora will want you there, too."

I assured myself that Wah would never leave Htet in order to join us in New York, though didn't I grasp, even then, that by attempting to lure Charlie my way I was doing some damage to their family? He'd only ever come to us when a conference justified his absence from them and paid his way.

It is not an exaggeration to say that I was elated when he flew in the following Saturday and rushed straight from the airport, through a barrage of traffic and rain, to the over-full hall where I was waiting in my seat between Nora and Milton, peering periodically over my shoulder in anxious expectation of him. Suddenly he was there, splendid and half soaked and standing within the rear entryway as he ran a hand through his hair and scanned the audience until he caught sight of me.

I still sometimes struggle to put my finger on what precisely about him was worth so much to Milton and me, why we should have each risked something as monumental as our marriage, or at least Milton's pride, to hold on to him. There aren't so many people anymore whose lives are about real connection, a real exchanging of ideas and revelations, even difficult ones. We have family, and we have our computers and phones and the things we do with them. But to be drawn into Charlie's world was to become part of a very deep and ongoing conversation, to be pulled along the currents of his innermost thoughts and conflicts, and to be attended to intimately in ways of the heart and mind—and soul, if I'm honest. I had only to send or say three or four words to him for the faucet of his intimacy to turn on. He was right there, his rushing closeness right there. And then suddenly it was not.

Following the ceremony, he found us in the crowd and pulled each of us in for a long, enveloping hug. Nora began to laugh in his arms, and Milton kept patting his side—to thank him, I imagine, for shouldering my good fortune alongside him. A strangely configured, yet somehow perfectly complete family of four.

Though nothing can remain perfect or pure for long, as Charlie might say. Soon enough at that reception we were drawn apart to mix with others. At one point, I took refuge at the bar only to spot Charlie and Nora, across the hall, engaged in conversation with a young editor I'd met at one of my publisher's holiday parties. The editor, Maia was her name, was the kind of fantastic-looking human one can only gape at in amazement; it didn't help that she'd been introduced to me as a "brilliant" writer in her own right. From a distance it was impossible to tell if Charlie was granting her his usual rapt attention or glutting himself on the unjust satisfactions of her beauty, but staring at them, I felt a panic that may not have been exempt from discriminatory envy. I hated the gorgeous splendor of her hair and the tawny hue of the clavicle she kept touching with a fingertip, never mind the way she was tipping her champagne glass toward Charlie's chest as though to describe some imagined, future joining of their bodies, all while poor Nora looked on, pinched and pale and anorexic by comparison—once again the girl on the periphery of others' insular games.

"She's enamored of you," I heard my editor say.

He'd swooped in to replace the glass in my hand and must have noticed the object of my tactless scrutiny; when I glanced up at his discerning eyes, hooded by the sprawling unruliness of his gray eyebrows, he inclined them obscurely in Maia's direction.

"Nora?" I tried, but he shot me a scowl, as though to communicate his expectation of nothing less than ruthless acuity from me. "Ah, Maia," I said, with an indifference whose tinny pretense rang in my ears. "I think you mean she's enamored of *him*."

"In other words, *you're* enamored."

105

"On the contrary, I'm disappointed. As we speak, he's succumbing to her betrayal of feminism—"

"Her *betrayal*—"

"Her use of beauty to excite his interest."

You know, I think that was the first time I'd seen my editor turn the measure of his offended gaze directly at me. With a worry that sobered me so much that I had to take a gulp of the drink he seemed suddenly to want to take away, he said, "She's exceptionally intelligent, Tessa . . . Be careful." And then: "If this is about your infatuation with your new friend, you might want to check it. Don't want to get into another mess of a marriage imploding."

Every time I have been lucky, the stroke of luck has served as a sort of stroke of a clock. Now the time has come for misfortune. For if happenstance is responsible for luck, and if luck brings a temporary feeling of satisfaction, luck can never provide meaning to a life. It can never drown out the noise of the thousand ticking clocks of the unlucky.

I remember standing alone in a daze at the reception, trying not to meet the eyes of the finalists who surely deserved the prize as much or more. And I remember realizing that I had lost track of Milton. Even now, I can recall only impressions of him on that day: the gentle squeeze he gave my elbow after I'd received the award and returned to my seat, the way he wandered alone through the crowds at the reception, how

I finally glimpsed him out on the patio, standing by himself in the falling darkness and speaking urgently into his phone. I think to have admitted to myself that he was suffering would have been to concede that I didn't know how to be his wife, no more than I'd known how to be Nick's.

But Charlie. Maia. Milton's call. Poor Nora and the alarmed look in her eyes that abated only a few hours on, when the four of us convened, along with my editor, around a celebratory table at our favorite little place in the East Village. It's terrible, but I can't recall where Milton was sitting during that meal. Charlie was positioned beside Nora and across from my editor, who was seated beside me . . . For a while, all seemed well again, more than well, my dread drowned out by the clatter and hum of the restaurant, and Nora's flushed looks of pleasure, and Charlie's confidence and loquaciousness. He was really in his best form that night, finally winning over my editor, who, after listening to his confessions about feeling estranged from Htet, began to ponder aloud about a future project on masculinity, a book Charlie might be just the scholar to write. Hearing that and hoping it might lead Charlie out of the wilderness of his vocational entanglements and isolation, I had the sense of arriving at a vantage point from which everything between us (including my irritation with his Don Juanian fixation on femininity) appeared to be justified. Our friendship wasn't an ill-fated exercise in mutual vanity, two egos' Sisyphean rehearsal of arrogant and blasphemous lines; rather, we were *getting* somewhere—if nowhere other than closer to a publishable articulation of his experience as a man.

Though sometime before the dinner plates were cleared, Nora began to tell the table about the support group she'd organized for adolescent girls at a middle school near Columbia. One girl, she said, had given her a scare by announcing to the group that all men did was abuse and insult and assault. The girl's own father wasn't so bad, or so the girl said—sometimes he yelled, but he was mostly at work and would never hurt anyone. It was just that it had gotten to the point, with everything she was hearing at school and on social media, where she didn't believe men were worth the risk of having around. When she passed a strange man on the street, what she saw was a possible rapist. It would be better, she said, if all men were dead.

"I've been telling Charlie about her for weeks," Nora told us at the conclusion of the story, a vague look of fear passing over her eyes as she glanced at me.

I've been telling Charlie about her for weeks?

As a waiter came around with wine, Charlie put a hand over his glass and maintained an easy smile, intent to assert his innocence, I thought. And had they really been communicating, he and Nora? Speaking on the phone or online? Why hadn't either of them told me?

"Obviously, I'm relieved women are finally speaking up about what it's like," Nora rambled on, almost to neutralize her disclosure, "the humiliations, the manipulations by men, the acts of violence. Obviously, I don't want women going back in the closet about any of that. But I'm worried about children, this girl." *I'm worried about the girl I was, about the girl I am*, she might have been saying. I don't know why my mind went there—everything seemed to be an accusation with her in those days. "Everything is so bleak. They're growing up on a dying planet without hope, a sick world filled with hateful people."

"Careful," I found myself instructing her, "or you'll sound like an assault apologist."

It was, my warning, an iteration of the one I'd given Charlie that night with the historian, and for a moment, the silence that overcame the table was so profound I seemed to hear the unfairness of my words reverberating in the air between us.

"Nora could never be at risk of that," my editor said, laughing, though Charlie frowned, as if he'd suddenly lost track of the easiness he'd been trying to project. I think it was then that I realized Milton had gone missing. He'd started the meal at one end of the table, I believe, but he'd kept vanishing, shifting around—to get the sight of me out of his eyes, maybe.

I nearly excused myself to go find him, but Charlie said something that stopped me: "You know, Tessa, I'm with Nora on this."

"It's all right," Nora told him. "My mother likes to be a contrarian. But she can't stand it when anyone else is."

The thousand ticking clocks of the unlucky . . .

But my heart was one of those, my miserable ticking heart. None of us spoke—Milton, Charlie, or I—in the rear of the car that drove us through another storm back to Brooklyn that night. The sound of the rain hitting the street seemed to augment the silence and loneliness in the car, and I kept trying to understand if Maia was responsible for ruining my mood or if the real problem was Wah, her having met Charlie before I'd had the chance to. It was tempting to believe that every misunderstanding between us could have been avoided if I'd married him instead of Nick.

Charlie had never stayed the night at our place in the city, and with a certain formality he took in the bedroom where we installed him and then asked if I wouldn't mind if he took a few minutes to freshen up before coming out to talk with me. Thinking about that place now—a gutted and modernized brownstone apartment that Milton and I had bought with a view to being empty nesters—I can't help but be chilled by its severity. I had wanted to showcase a sparseness that is often elusive to parenthood. Nora hadn't ever really lived with us, as I've said, and when Milton's boys departed for college one by one, it had been a relief to attain a line of sight there uninterrupted by pizza boxes and binders and cleats, nagging material reminders of our responsibility for them.

I'd left an oversized robe for Charlie in the bathroom, and out of some misunderstanding, or perhaps just the contrary, he came out to the darkened living room wearing it, his wet hair combed back and his skin—I noticed as I passed him a cup of herbal tea—smelling of the verbena soap I'd put by the tub. I don't mean to suggest that he looked like a man on the verge of seducing me. Rather, he could have been a close relative, totally relaxed as he sank into the seat across from mine with that same expression of gratification I'd glimpsed when he'd first taken in the expanse of the farm. But my heart was racing.

I thought I might have the courage to bring up Nora's revelation about their communications—whatever they'd been—though suddenly I was afraid of the truths we were keeping, and instead I said, "Tell me about Joaquin." I don't think I'd quite realized until that moment that I'd been unable to rid my concerns about that young man from my conceptions of Charlie, or, rather, that I'd been attempting to chasten my feelings for Charlie with my concerns about Joaquin. Oh, I know Charlie could also be hard on the girl; but she was a survivor, and the young man seemed to me to be so gravely at risk.

I've already told you about the force of Charlie's gaze, how large his eyes grew when he was making a case or trying to comprehend something, how intent he seemed, as though his ferocity were rushing up to meet you, to take you within those two apertures where transference between the world and his essence met the least resistance. It was those eyes that fixed on me now, across the dimness.

"What do you want to know?" he said, almost defensively. And then, after setting his tea on the table between us: "He used to work for the man who bought the place next to ours."

"The Victorian?"

I saw him nod and turn his gaze to the walnut bank of windows facing the street—the room's only concession to warmth—as though to seek out something in them or in the greater night that he wasn't finding in me.

"A flipper," he explained. "He's been trying to fix it on the cheap, without permits, and the preservationists keep shutting him down. Meanwhile, the house is in peril. People like Joaquin taking shelter in it. No gas, no electricity, so they're lighting fires, leaving garbage. I keep telling Duane—"

"Duane?"

"The flipper. People assume he's a child of the neighborhood, but he grew up in the Antelope Valley. Not in a rush to finish the house and get his money out, I guess."

"And Wah?" I remembered her idea for a book about the neighborhood, and a kind of shame about my private disparagement of it made me want to prove that not even she was innocent in this little tale of speculation and greed.

Charlie wrapped his hands around his tea and held it up near his chest, so that I had the impression, again, that he was seeking out a warmth he couldn't—perhaps hadn't ever been able to—find in the living. Children, all of us, wanting the heat and safety of a mother's embrace. "Wah's concern is Htet," he said, with an air of estrangement not entirely free of tenderness, "and Htet understands Joaquin. He's been homeless since Duane fired him. So Wah feeds him, intercedes with Duane, the police, tries to get him work, a place to live. And she turns a blind eye whenever he shows up again at the house, ignoring me when I tell her it's dangerous—not least of all for the kid himself."

I asked him what would happen to Joaquin, and a guilty expression descended over his face, so that I worried he'd already had the Victorian padlocked and the boy carted off to juvenile hall.

But he only said, "He'll be fine." And then: "Wah will make sure that he, at least, is fine. And Htet." He thought a moment. "Have I told you about Nietzsche's bow?"

Today I understand that Nietzsche is for Charlie what Camus has been for me: an imperfect human filter, a way of seeing the world more clearly and measuring its breadth and beauty without looking up toward God or down from imagined heavenly heights, and also a way of dismantling the heavy scales of justice we're all so enamored of these days. When I put Camus himself on those scales, the fact that he womanized and cheated on his wife outweighs, will always outweigh, the good he did because crimes always outweigh good—that is the rule of the scale. If a crime and a good are of equal weight, the crime takes the day. Still, when I look at something through the filter of Camus's work and thought, my view becomes more tolerant of aberration, complexity. "I don't believe so," I said—a truth, but also a lie, for Charlie had told the story of Nietzsche's bow to Nora during their brief walk through the drizzle on the morning of their meeting at the farm, and Nora had subsequently told the story to me.

"Nietzsche was writing *The Antichrist*," Charlie said now, his head shooting around to the walnut bank of windows again, almost as though to check if we weren't in fact being watched by a higher being. "And one evening he goes to the home of close friends, where at a certain point the wife takes him aside and says she understands he's writing something that's critical of Christianity, and she reveals—the wife—that she's thinking of giving up her faith. What does Nietzsche do? Breaks down, starts to weep, says, 'Don't give up your great idea.' The woman's truth was that God might not exist, that Christianity might be a construct built around a fundamental fallacy, but to embrace that truth, to give up her great idea of God, would be to deprive herself of the value of her faith, the beauty and comfort and dignity it brought to her life. So, on the one side there is *truth* for Nietzsche, on the other *value*. Two ends of a bow—the kind you'd use to shoot an arrow. And our mandate is to live with both ends in tension, to pull the bow taut, never succumbing to the temptation to relent to one extreme or the other—all truth or all value. Nietzsche called it 'the magnificent tension of the spirit.' And with this tension, our arrow might one day hit its target; we might overcome, *be*come who we are."

When Nora had conveyed the same story to me, she'd added that she and Charlie had been discussing Yash, the boyfriend who had broken her heart the previous night with another cruel appraisal of her idiosyncrasies. I'd asked her what horrible thing Yash had told her this time, but she wouldn't answer me, only said, "I told Charlie I was done with Yash, and he asked if I was holding him to too high a standard. What does Charlie expect, women to lower their standards to make men feel better about being assholes? I asked Charlie that, and he told me I was your daughter all right. And when I told him what Yash had said, he said, 'You're right, he *is* an asshole.' And I told him I felt like I'd wasted another six months of my life. That's when he said, 'There is no safe love.'"

"Don't give up your great idea," Charlie continued now, his eyes intently studying me across the dim space.

"What great idea?" I asked him. *What great idea are you telling me not to give up—my fantasy of you, of us?* His look had become so open, it made me want to cover my face and hide.

"In *Midlife*," he started, and still he gazed at me with that frightening forthrightness, "you describe the midlife crisis as a rebellion against the perceived oppressive conditions of one's life." I wasn't sure if he was asking a question or making a point, and the attentive pause he fell into was like a lure I saw myself breathlessly following. "What if you can't see your conditions as anything but oppressive?"

I was still too occupied by the manifold directions that his line of thought might take to answer right away. "Perception is changeable," I finally tried—to test him, I think. Or to test the direction of my own stifled inclinations, the limits of my courage. "But you have to *want* it to change, *want* to see the value of another perspective. That's something women do all the time, exert powerful control over their perspective in order to maintain the status quo. Will themselves to view their relationship in the best possible light, particularly if they have a family, to preserve the form of the relationship, one that benefits the family, if not them specifically."

His face had become very still, almost fixed, his eyes still trained on mine, so that with horror I seemed to see my own rapt interest reflected in them, to be laid bare. And yet that mirror of his gaze induced in me a sense of vertigo, so that I felt not only exposed but sick. I couldn't seem to control my perspective on anything, least of all of him.

And with dizziness I perceived him saying, "But you didn't do that. You didn't will yourself to see your first husband in the best light to preserve what you had. Were you in love with someone else when you left him?"

"Why would you ask that?"

"All your writing about Camus's infidelity. I can't help reading something personal in it, as if you're arguing yourself out of something. And the lines of his you quote—'Why should it be essential to love rarely in order to love much?'"

Why should it be essential to love only Wah and not also you?

It wasn't true that I'd strayed when married to Nick, yet hadn't I yearned for something more than I'd ever permitted either of us? I'd yearned to be challenged, to be held accountable for my habit of coldness and self-defense. I'd yearned to give more of myself. But I'd never managed to respect Nick enough for that. He was a paper doll version of everything my parents hadn't been: cautious, deferential. And Nick's greatest attempt to become a man to my fledgling woman had sent me ripping him to shreds.

"What are you saying?" I sputtered. "That you want to jump ship? Stopped valuing your marriage? That—that there's someone else?"

I'm not sure how I hoped he would answer as he sat there, half naked before me. Only not as he did.

"You don't have to stop valuing a marriage," he said, "to see the truth that you want to end it."

10.

ND HERE WE ARE, careening toward the end of everything as it was between us.

I didn't throw myself at Charlie in my cold living room
that night. Didn't demand to know what was going on with
Nora or why he wanted to leave his wife. I believed this left
me safe—morally, even—as though remaining in the realm
of fantasy exempted me from guilt, responsibility. Well, it
did nothing of the kind.

About two weeks after the awards ceremony, Milton
surprised me by announcing that he'd booked an anniversary
trip for us to Palm Springs. The plan, he said with a pallid
trepidation I couldn't help noting, was to fly into Los Angeles and stay with Charlie for a night before being joined by
him, and maybe Wah, for a more leisurely visit in the desert.
I didn't mention the oddness of spending our anniversary
with others; both of us knew, I think, that we were no longer

enough alone—or, rather, that our excitement together was being sustained, if also complicated, by *them*.

Because Htet had a holiday choral concert at her school on the evening of our arrival, no one was home when we pulled onto their darkening street, and I took in everything that had changed: the state of the freshly boarded-up Victorian, in whose dusky driveway sat a gleaming black pickup truck; the way various houses were strung up with lights, some beginning to twinkle even as we maneuvered around for a parking space; and the trees, their trunks unvaryingly wrapped in foil and factory-pressed Christmas bows, many of their branches shorn of leaves so that the place appeared not just cheapened but naked and defenseless, more subject to the unremitting and now unmuffled roar of the nearby freeway.

And yet not everything was changed. As we pulled our bags down the cold sidewalk, we passed Ernie and that American flag hanging limply from the pole on his lawn. He was nestled on his porch with a glass of red wine, and though I nodded to him—we still hadn't been formally introduced—and he held a trembling hand up to me, the blank look on his face did not waver, not even when Milton and I began to fumble and fight with the lockbox on a spigot between the properties.

"What a strange old man," I told Milton, once our break-in was complete and we'd dropped our bags in the living room.

There was an unfamiliar smell about the place without the family present. I was taken again by how barren its shadowed rooms seemed and had the feeling that its few pieces of furniture were vigilantly standing guard, ready to report on us in defense of Wah.

"Think I'll have a shower," Milton said. I suppose my comment about Ernie had been mean. "Dinner at eight," he added, heading up the stairs with our bags. The plan was for the others to drop off Htet at the house before we made our collective way to a restaurant downtown that Charlie had been wanting to try.

For a few minutes I remained there, observing the living room's shaded, velvety walls. It was a quiet house, perhaps even a weary house, yet I couldn't help sensing, what with the casement windows on every side, that the place was in gentle thrall to the surrounding landscape, to the fading breath of day and last, plant-touched light, each window an eye to the natural. And I had the thought that in taking such care with the exterior plantings, Wah had been feeding the house's hunger, nourishing its soul, if you like. And yet the thought didn't satisfy me.

When I was a young child, not more than six, the same friend who persuaded me to stone the crow led me to a house on a block between ours. The memory is so buried that I can recall it only with the glowing indefiniteness of a dream. I have no idea anymore why we passed through the front door, which may have been slightly ajar or unlocked. What I remember is discovering that no one was home. And the stillness of the place, the undisturbed furnishings, the light, all of it lying in wait for someone who was not me. *I am not meant to be here. They could come back and find me.* Those were the ideas behind my quivering sense of prohibition and something else—a feeling that I had stumbled onto some unknown region of myself where connection with others' private lives became possible. I was so alone in my own home, and here the secret selves of others seemed so close.

I believe my childhood friend and I repeated that act of unconsented entry with one or two other houses around the same time. We were never caught, nor did I touch a thing. All I ever wanted was to *see*. And now, with the squeak of Milton's shower starting, I seemed to follow that same little girl up the staircase, whose width and grandeur under the second floor's vaulted ceiling suddenly daunted me.

Their door was just beyond the landing, its iron knob letting out a whine when turned. Then I was taking in their room, barren and antique white in the light of the yellow ceiling lamp, with the same cathedral vaulting that seemed to comment on the sanctity of something—of their world together, which I was even then desecrating. Their bed lay on the floor, its ink-stained coverlet arrayed with books and Charlie's philosophy journals, his glasses, his jeans. In the corner stood a bookshelf piled with folded laundry, and beside it was the closet, its door opening onto hanging garments so widely spaced apart that I experienced a pang of envy, or shame. But it was to the table across from me that I was drawn. It faced the rear garden's acacia tree, the falling night, and on its marred surface sat a laptop, papers, bills, and—I saw once I was close enough to touch the laptop's metal lid—a photograph of young Htet, dressed in the frilly white garb of a Catholic confirmation ceremony. Wah wasn't *Christian*, was she?

The question made me aware, for some reason, of my compromised position, and I had the terrible sensation of being watched, of some soul staring up into the bright window at my prying face. I decided to switch off the light when suddenly a banging erupted over the hiss of Milton's shower—someone pounding on the door downstairs. Could it be Joaquin, I wondered, or even the police, summoned by some neighbor who'd seen me? Telling myself that I was being paranoid, I took my time descending to the door and opening it.

I'd never seen the balding man standing under the porch light, though I guessed soon enough that he might be Duane—the flipper, as Charlie had described him. He was holding a bulky contractor's trash bag in his fist. And there was nothing neighborly about his proprietary stare, the irritated depths of which fell down the length of my body before predictably losing interest in my curves' minor eventualities.

"Is there something I can help you with?" I asked, after explaining that Wah and Charlie were out.

His response was resonant with insinuation. "You're one of *Charlie's* friends."

I conceded that I was, that my husband and I were guests at the house for the night. *Husband*: the word threw a kind of electric spark as I uttered it, as if I were acknowledging an impediment to my potential illicit coupling with my "friend" Charlie, or even with him, this sturdy and brooding stranger before me.

"You can tell him I did what he wanted," he said. "Boarded up everything real good. That kid won't be coming back." He held up the bag, almost to dare me to take it. "Wah asked me to save his things. I'll put this by her trash so she can do what she likes with it."

He turned away with the bag as if to leave, but at the porch steps he stopped, casting a troubled look back at me.

"I'm Duane," he said, and when I began to say my name, he interrupted: "I know who you are. Wah told me about you. Said Charlie wanted me to finish up this afternoon because you were coming."

Have you ever experienced the phenomenon of meeting a man who expects you to be attracted to him, only to find yourself unwittingly trying to attract him in turn? Why in God's name had I sucked in my gut as that stranger, Duane,

helped himself to an evaluation of my body's meager offer-
ings? Standing before the misty mirror after a shower and
applying products to my face, I seemed to be assembling a
crude image of self-possession over a roiling mess of mind.
Or, rather: the roiling mess of the woman I am in reality.

It was close to eight, the living room dim when Milton
and I sat on the stiff sofa trying to read, counting down the
minutes until the family returned and we adults could head
out to that dinner, for which we were already running late.
"Shouldn't we push back the reservation?" I said.

Then suddenly there they were, Charlie and Wah without the girl, unlatching the door and entering in a cloud of
agitation, as if they hadn't quite arrived where they wanted
to be or were in recovery from some squabble during the
car ride. Charlie looked confused when Milton leaped up to
make a joke about welcoming them back to their own place.
But a moment later he caught on and, feigning surprise, asked
what we were doing there—an effort that fell flat.

And there was something distinctly off about the way
Wah faced us. I'd never seen the belted blue tunic she wore,
so short that it made her legs, already drawn out by dark
tights and heels, seem half a foot longer. Milton gave a little
start when she stepped toward us—I think not even he had
thought she could appear so statuesque. But it wasn't this
transformation or even the effort behind it that distressed me
so much as what she'd done with her eyes. They were lined

and smudged in black like Htet's, so that when she turned her gaze gently to me I had the feeling of being smacked.

"Htet decided to spend some time with a friend," she said, with a hint of defensiveness. Maybe she was bothered by our never having found a way to interact comfortably with the girl.

"Let's get going," Charlie said, as if to brush all that aside.

He was in a state, Charlie. En route to the restaurant, when the freeway congestion entrapping the car seemed to be rivaled by our climbing tension within it, I was aware that he wasn't presently the man I'd come so much to enjoy, that the man behind the wheel—the one who kept honking and jerking the car this way and that—was the reactive, insecure Charlie I'd gleaned in those early letters and over dinner with the historian, the Charlie who couldn't shake his philosophical arguments against the injustices of our times, who felt himself so menaced that he had little left to give to his family, or to me. And when he dumped us in front of a grimy Beaux Arts building downtown, waving off the valet while Milton skittered around to the front passenger seat to help him look for cheaper parking, I felt like someone in the process of being left for good.

It didn't help that, when Wah turned to me with an apologetic shake of her head, I noticed a valet's attention being coopted by her short blue dress. Nor did it help that in the elevator, whose creaks were so persistent I feared we'd be sent crashing to our deaths, the only other occupant—a grinning, paunchy businessman—went out of his way to ask Wah a question about whether reservations upstairs were necessary.

And so it went: the deepening of my sense of invisibility, of being disregarded, and the concomitant awakening of my attentiveness to Wah's charms. Even the host who seated us, a thin, affected nugget of cuteness, as I'd heard Nora describe someone back in her relatively freer collegiate days, seemed to take conspiratorial pleasure in joking with Wah about latecomers being the kind of patrons he preferred to seat ("Punctual people can be so entitled, don't you think?").

"Dry martini," I told a plainer and more harried young gentleman, our server, after we'd settled into a corner of the rooftop patio outside. "No—dirty. Dirty vodka martini."

"I think I'll wait to order something," Wah told the man calmly. She could have done the decent thing and joined me in having a drink.

For a few minutes we sat in silence, absorbing the cacophonous soundscape and vast night views of downtown L.A., its illumined assortment of new and tarnished buildings, until she offered up some words about the trajectory of a nearby deco masterpiece across the square below.

"Duane came by this afternoon," I interrupted. I suppose I wanted to cut through to a more personal difficulty.

The candle flickering between us accentuated the concern overcoming Wah's face, the mix-up of her reticence and knowing. "I hope he was friendly," she said, so that I wondered if I should mention the *especially* friendly way Duane had eyed me. But she added, "He can be brusque sometimes. I don't think he feels welcome on the street."

To my advantage, or perhaps to hers, the server swooped in with the martini, and Wah watched as I helped myself to a generous mouthful of the overly briny drink. When I'd set down the glass, she asked whether Duane had wanted anything in particular.

"Only to say *you* wanted something," I told her, letting her wonder what I meant for a moment before explaining about the trash bag of Joaquin's things. It was strange, the way she stared at me as I spoke, almost as though she couldn't make out my words over the shouts and guffaws of a boisterous group on the patio's far side, or as though the intoxication already touching my brain were showing on my lips, which I began to dab at with my napkin.

"Would you mind not mentioning all that to Charlie?" she said at last, and began to explain that Duane had been willing to overlook Joaquin staying in the place while it was sitting empty, so long as the young man didn't leave trash for others to clean, whereas Charlie's priority was Htet's safety. "He thinks Htet needs to be protected," she added.

"And she doesn't?" I asked, even as I couldn't imagine that ferocious girl—a model of strength—needing anything like Charlie's protection.

"Of course. She's still a child. But she was independent for so long. And it's not going to work if she thinks Charlie's being heartless with Joaquin. If it's *all* about protecting her, our house, our interests. When your life is reduced to that . . . self-interest, survival . . . If there hadn't been others for her to protect when she was young, other children—if all she'd done in Malaysia was keep herself alive—the thing that makes her Htet would have died."

"And what is that—'the thing that makes her Htet'?" I was, at that point, still as interested in her perspectives on the girl as I was increasingly driven to contest them for reasons that escaped me.

Wah looked at me with genuine surprise. "Well—her heart," she said finally. "Her capacity to care for others." But her earnestness had the tenor of a slight, as though she'd really said, *Despite all that's happened to her, she's not so inhuman, my daughter, as to be heartless like you.* "I've been taking Htet to a therapist through our university," she continued. "I don't know if you remember recommending that I get her into therapy . . . A very caring woman. But what she has to teach Htet is so *Western.*"

Certainly, I remembered the morning she'd told me about Htet wanting to pay that pedophile back, when I'd urged her to get the girl into therapy, and she'd gone on to accuse me of ordinary thinking. And now as she proceeded to rattle out a litany of the psychoanalytic Westernisms that she took issue with—*no good comes to martyrs; it's all about you; self-care isn't selfish*—I explored the dregs of my drink, trying to drown my rising indignation. Was this little condemnatory speech actually meant as an argument against me, against my "ordinary" Western notions? "As if you're weak or pathetic if you prioritize giving to others," she was saying. "As if you're doomed. But that's the strongest thing about Htet—her desire to be of assistance."

"Is it?" I fired back. "She seems to me to be the model of independence, gusto." *Why are you making your daughter into a feminine stereotype?* I nearly added.

But the men were suddenly upon us, dropping themselves into their seats. I raised my empty glass to them as they carried on with some conversation about one of Charlie's old friends—an opera critic they'd just run into on the corner, who'd nearly convinced them to steal away to the performance of *Pagliacci* he was about to see up the street.

Milton must have sensed my displeasure at that, because after we'd read out our orders to the server, he added a bottle of champagne and another cocktail for me and said to the table, his face flushing, "You know this is our seventh anniversary? I met Tessa when I was still married to Kathleen."

"*Milton*," I said. I'd never told Charlie of the circumstances under which my second marriage had come to be.

Milton looked dazed, as if I'd ruined his high. "Why can't I talk about how you saved me?" he said, and turned back to the others. "With Kathleen, everything had to be negotiated, every detail of the boys' lives. We became a firm representing them—that's what it felt like. Imagine the relief of being with Tessa, someone apart from all that suffocating minutiae. It didn't matter anymore that the boys had their hockey or that Nora hated being at the farm—if the two of us needed to be there, Tessa and I, if we needed that time together, we *went*."

"Yes," I said, that sick feeling in my veins again. "We did. And you said, 'Leave her.'"

"I what?"

"You said, 'Leave her'—*Nora*. 'It'll be good for her,' you told me. 'It'll make her independent.' 'She needs to learn the world doesn't revolve around her.'"

For a moment, Milton studied me with that same bewildered look, his smile half fallen. "Exactly," he said, hesitance in his eyes as he cast them around the table again. "And isn't that exactly the problem with the young these days? Their feelings always being hurt? Their pride always being offended? Their sense that the world should revolve around their ideas and needs? Nora's not like that, neither are the boys—"

"Because we prioritized ourselves?" I said.

"That's right." When he faced me now, it was with the beginnings of a scowl. "You're the one who taught me that a person should do that."

Nothing was right, not the effects on my blood of the second martini that I downed nearly as soon as it came, nor the way Charlie wouldn't meet my gaze, nor Wah's stupid look of sympathy, how she kept seeking out my face to read it with that intolerable expression of feeling and pity. It was just a story, Milton's account of the beginnings of our marriage. A story justifying our crime of adultery. No truer than the story he'd probably told himself when he'd left someone else for Kathleen. If Nora had been correct at the ramen house when she'd accused me of being a make-believe artist with no hold on my own reality, Milton was also one in his way.

I suppose I couldn't keep pretending. Pretending that I liked everyone at that table. That we wanted to nurture something like domestic peace rather than war. "Charlie," I said, and he looked at me with surprise, as though he didn't expect to find me still sitting at the table across from him. "I had the chance to meet Duane earlier."

It was remarkable, the difference between how Charlie and Wah digested that. She seemed almost to have expected I'd bring up Duane despite her request that I avoid mentioning him, whereas what I'd said hardly seemed to register with Charlie, who proceeded to flag down the server and ask if we couldn't get some olives or bread while we were waiting for the food to arrive.

"Another martini?" the server asked me, and I nodded with resignation and shame.

"Duane came by the house," I tried again, five or ten minutes on, when that third, fortifying martini finally came.

"Probably looking for Wah," Charlie said, popping an olive between his lips. "He loves her."

"Does he?"

"He *doesn't love* me," Wah said, and I noticed that Milton was draining his own glass of champagne.

"The other day," Charlie said, "Duane stops me as I'm pulling out the trash cans and says, 'It's good to see you doing some work for your wife.' Another time we're walking to the car, and he says, 'You better be good to your woman, because I'll be the first on your porch if she kicks you out.'" A different man might have been upset at Duane, or bragging by sharing his eagerness to step in, but Charlie looked like he'd been let off the hook.

"What a letch," I said.

"It's just Duane's way," Wah said.

"I saw his way," I snapped at her. "I saw it when he came to the door and leered at me. A letch. You should have slapped him."

She cringed, as though I'd suggested she were the one who should have been slapped. And I guess I thought she did deserve to be. With all that martini in me, I had the idea that her excusing Duane was as disgusting as his treating her like an object to be traded.

"I prefer to try to understand where people are coming from," she said.

"*Where people are coming from?*" There was a burble of drunkenness in my voice.

"He was probably trying to pay me a compliment."

I saw her throw a glance at Charlie, maybe to see if he'd jump in, but he'd become very quiet, sitting back in his chair, his eyes moving between us as though he couldn't decide which one of us to save.

"I'll tell you what," I found myself telling Wah. "Beauty— the beauty you believe that man was trying to compliment—"

"I didn't mean anything about looks," she said with embarrassment.

"You didn't? But aren't you suggesting that your attractiveness to Duane should be held accountable for his actions? Isn't it like that man—that *pedophile* your daughter wants to pay back? *Poor* man," I said with mock sympathy, "helplessly seduced by her little-girl body—"

"Tessa—" Milton cut in, while Wah stared at me with those large, astounded eyes.

"You don't need to save her," I barked at him now. "Despite her behaving like a frightened girl, Wah's not a child who needs protection." With a certain horror, martini in hand, I saw myself begin to clutch at my chest, acting out the part of a helplessly enfeebled girl. "*Please help me,*" I said. "*Save me. I'm so delicate. Please like me. Keep thinking I'm pretty.*"

Some of my martini sloshed across my stomach and lap, and I dabbed at it with the napkin as though to sop up my spite, while another version of myself argued inwardly that the spite was justified, that I was merely acting in the service of women: How, really, could we hope to advance as a sex if we allowed ourselves to play into men's fantasies and interests to such an extent?

Your reasoning is ordinary.

"A woman's attractiveness to a man is *ordinary*," I declared, thrusting the martini glass onto the table. "It's boring, excuses nothing, exonerates no one. Especially not the woman who ordinarily cultivates it."

"Jesus Christ," Milton said.

And still Charlie was silent, his gaze shifting between us.

"Don't you see?" I said to Wah over the restaurant's din, nearly shouting. "When you stand by and allow a man to demean you and others by association, when you laugh it off and explain it away and even *enjoy* it, you become—" What would have happened, I wonder, if the mother of my crow-hating friend hadn't stopped us from finishing off our dismal task? To stop stoning the crow of our own accord, we would have had to reckon with our errors of perception. We would have had to fathom the possibility of forgiving ourselves for our wrongs. It was so much easier to continue believing that the crow was unforgivably bad, to see its punishment through to our righteous end. I am not bad: *you* are

135

bad. I am not wrong: *you* are wrong. *You* are wrong. *You are wrong . . .* "—an *insult to womankind.*"

And here we are, back to where I started this story. Unfortunately, it's not where my tirade ended. If it had ended there, the only casualty might have been Wah's willingness to tolerate anything more to do with me. But after she went on to tell me, in a quavering voice, that I'd misunderstood her (as mentioned at the beginning of this confession of meanness), and after I'd answered, "I think not," and proceeded to argue that I saw a frightening connection between a girl's need to be liked and a woman's need to please men, a thought took hold of me. Or rather, an image, one I'd spied earlier on her desk: that of young Htet in her frilly white confirmation dress. And, staring into Wah's wounded eyes now, I straightened my spine and announced, with a staid finality meant to suggest that this deliberation we'd been having had come to an end: "There is no *God* who will reward you for your softness, Wah. There is no 'Kingdom of Heaven' that will reward your pathetic attempts at tolerance and your suffering of others' slights."

A wince of surprise passed over her face, followed by something else. Pity maybe.

"There is, at least," she said, "my conscience."

But I had won. I saw it in the tears that finally sprang to her eyes and that she visibly refused to shed.

I'll never forget Milton's harrowed look as he stared at me then. It was a look that said, *If I still held you in a certain trust until a moment ago, now the precious membrane of our togetherness has been irretrievably torn.* And suddenly he swung around to Wah and reached for her hand and said, "I'll tell you what, I consider you to be incredibly strong. Incredibly strong. And if something were to happen to Tessa and me, I'd come straight to you for support."

I turned to Charlie, who appeared so lost and confused, so broken, he could have been the one I'd been pummeling all along. "You should tell them," I instructed him. "Tell *her*."

When he couldn't seem to make out what I meant, I shifted around to Wah, her hand still in Milton's. "He wants to leave you."

I thought Charlie was going to say something finally. He made a gurgling noise and opened his mouth, as if to corroborate what I'd come out with. But his face went pale. He pushed his chair out from the table and stood. And just like that, he walked away.

For a minute, we all sat watching him weave through the patio tables. Then he disappeared behind a crowd of bargoers inside.

"There," I said, looking back at the others. But I was swallowing my next three words: "I've done it."

11.

I NEVER THOUGHT OF THIS AS A STORY of faith, though I imagine you did when you asked me to write it. For all Charlie's Don Juanian will to wander and Nietzschean abhorrence of asceticism, he was helplessly attracted to Wah's devotional and spiritual side. People confuse the virtue for the fault, or the other way around. I suppose you could say the Christian mindset was the great problem of Charlie's life: he hated its value of self-sacrifice, even as he benefited from it and used it to his own ends, half destroying a soul he admired because she embodied it. But where, really, is the line between those "feminine" virtues of nurturing and gentleness that he was so enticed by and the Christian ones of service and self-sacrifice? Perhaps one day, after you've read all this, you can explain something about that to me.

None of us spoke much as we searched the bar and then the block for Charlie. I can't recall the precise choreography of Milton's directing me, in my vodka-addled state, to the spot on the street where he and Charlie had found parking. What remains is the memory of sitting alone on the rear seat as Wah drove us home. I stared at her profile and at the back of Milton's head, a feeling of weakness overcoming me, of dependency and shame, and it seemed to me obliquely that I had lived in error all my life. Wah hadn't really reacted to Charlie's leaving, only soldiered through our futile search for him with a vaguely tearful smile on her lips, as if his vanishing were some sad joke between them, a joke that was now on me. And as she steered the car down a highway so empty and hushed it seemed to be complying with her resolute peace, I kept trying to avert my gaze from her cheek, trying and failing, and feeling that she and Milton were two adults who shared a perspective or a rectitude that I would never be able to possess.

At the house, Wah let us in and disappeared upstairs, and soon Milton slouched up without bothering to look back at me. I stood alone in the living room, listening for Charlie. I kept thinking he must have found his way back by then and let himself in.

When finally I ascended to the guest room, I found Milton sitting with a stunned expression at the edge of the bed, his face reddened, hair askew, as though he'd briefly lain down and bolted up again, meaning to attend to something that had already slipped his mind. It happens just like that, doesn't it: someone vital and middle-aged turns into an old man? And I had done it to him. I had finally done it. Though here I am, reverting to the misogynist cliché that the source of a man's destruction is too often a difficult woman.

"I wonder how it feels," he said, as soon as I'd shut the door behind me.

"How *what* feels?"

"To be so sure of yourself." He wasn't looking at me. He was looking at the closet door in front of him. "What do you like to say, 'men ensnare women'?"

"I don't know what you mean." I went to the bag I hadn't unpacked and began to peel off the jeans I'd worn, so that suddenly I felt aware of my nakedness before him, my body's areas of softness overtaking those other parts still obedient to my determined thinness.

"She's not your enemy," I heard him say.

"No, she isn't."

"You don't need to be intimidated."

"Intimidated?"

"You're an intelligent woman, Tessa," he said, turning to me, "and it occurs to me that I've just stood by and allowed you—both of us—to hurt her and her marriage."

"She's not a child, Milton, as I said tonight."

"No," he answered, almost wistfully. "She's not a child. And you had no business treating her like one."

"And you had no business professing your love to her tonight."

"I wasn't—" he tried. "I didn't intend—"

But it was useless. That stunned look that I'd seen on his face when I'd come into the room passed over his eyes again, and for a moment he turned back to the closet, as though to escape to it.

"What I was sitting here thinking," he said finally, "is that we have no business being together."

"You've had too much to drink. You'll feel better after you've slept it off. We both will."

He looked at me again and took in my shape, my naked legs, my panties, my breasts beneath the top I was still wearing. How hideous I was; that's what I told myself, at least.

"What is it?" I said.

"Will you bite my head off if I say you're beautiful?"

For some reason, that was enough to make me shove my legs back into the jeans. *Unworthy, unworthy*—the word kept firing in my mind, though if its target was him or me, I wasn't sure.

"Where are you going?" he asked when I started for the door.

And I lied: "It will be better in the morning."

*   *   *

I didn't return to Milton that night. When I came downstairs the living room was empty, and the quiet and the stillness that had fallen over the house told me that Charlie was gone, that he may have left permanently, and that his leaving was obliquely related to how I'd left and left and left throughout my life. Left Nick and Nora. Left Mother and Dad. Left every lover or friend or family member whose scrutiny had become too unbearable to sustain. And now Milton. I would be leaving him, too, wouldn't I?

But, as if to leave my ugliness and unacceptability instead, I opened the front door and stepped out onto the porch where Duane had stood earlier. I seemed to be seeking something or someone I'd inadvertently left outside. Charlie, yes, but also a better version of myself, a nobler, more self-sufficient and poised version who would surely make everything all right. Yet the massed darkness of Wah's wooded garden beyond the porch, its sullen branches and smell of inner-city wildness, finally sent me back inside.

Vainly, I waited again for Charlie in the living room before it occurred to me that he could have sought refuge in his office, out on the barn's upper floor. And not knowing what it was I wanted more—to find him or to hide myself away—I let myself out the kitchen door and braved the gloom of Wah's backyard, the scuttle of creatures in the

143

brush. The barn, too, was dark and vacant looking, though as I approached the exterior staircase leading up to the old converted hayloft, a motion-activated floodlight shot down on me, so that I had the sense of evading the forces of security while proceeding up the steps and trying the door.

It was unlocked, but Charlie was not inside. I had never been in his office before, and after I stumbled to a nearby table and switched on a lamp, I was surprised by the disorder of the place, its dust balls and unmade cot and spider webbing and heaps of things—not only books and papers and files, but also clothes and old towels and an array of snacks and cans of food and drinks. How many hours had he banished himself to *this*, this private sanctuary, I wondered as I sank down onto the cot by the table and switched off the lamp, finally hiding beneath a tatty blanket that smelled of something comforting and clean.

Nowhere to sleep, I thought.

Or maybe the thought only came later, a few minutes or hours on, when the door creaked open and, waking, I heard myself call Charlie's name. Though almost immediately I saw someone else beyond the doorway—the young man, Joaquin, standing in the floodlight, an alert expression on his frightened face. He was peering blindly into the room, which was dark and must have mostly concealed me. Not a muscle in his body moved, not even when the roar of a passing plane began to intensify above him and a dog started barking in the alley as if to pin him up there with me. He was holding something—Duane's trash bag, I saw. Wah must have gotten word to him about the flipper coming by with his things. Maybe she'd urged him to sleep up here if he needed to, what with the Victorian shut up and Charlie gone.

He turned back toward the stairwell, making a warning motion, but a moment later, I heard someone bounding up; then Htet was there, standing breathlessly beside him under the floodlight, a spark of violence in her dark and beautiful face.

"What the fuck?" she said, squinting into the shadows toward me.

She yanked Joaquin into the room and flicked on the light, shutting the door behind them before reeling around with a wild look of accusation as he stood by mutely. I'd never noticed it before, how silencing she could be, her every indignant and protective glance that of a bully—maybe of *the* bullies who'd tormented her earlier days.

Well, I must have been a sorry sight, lying there in the clothes I'd worn to dinner, my hair a mess and my makeup smeared and that tatty blanket draped around my jeans. None of that was the real source of my shame, though. The real source was . . . I didn't know exactly. Not yet, anyway.

"What are you doing here?" she said to me.

"It's okay," Joaquin tried. He hefted the bag, making to leave, but she held out her arm to stop him.

"This lady," she said, "probably got into some fight with her man. Probably has hurt feelings. Thinks she can take what she likes." She seemed to see something—some deficit of feeling—in my face. "What's wrong with you? Why aren't you leaving? You can't have *everything*."

"I know," I answered, a waver in my voice.

It seemed I'd always known just that—that I didn't belong, that it was time to leave. I stood with the blanket clutched to my waist, but realizing I was making a mistake, I stopped to place the thing back on the cot for Joaquin.

"I'm going," I said to reassure them. It was stupid, the way a part of me still hoped they would stop me, welcome me.

Joaquin cast a concerned look my way as I proceeded toward the door, straightening my hair in embarrassment.

But she drew him closer to her as I neared. "My mom thinks this lady's fucking Charlie," she told him. "She's not his type. Too old. Skinny." And when I hesitated: "Bitch. Can't you see my friend needs to sleep?"

12.

SEVERAL MONTHS PASSED before I saw or heard from Charlie again. Because Milton and I had assiduously avoided another confrontation with the business of our marriage since that last night at the Craftsman, we were together in bed when the email from Charlie came through, so cryptic I can't bring myself to reproduce it here for fear of painting Charlie as more callous than he really was.

There had been a tragedy, he said—a fire at the Victorian—and Wah had died. Services would be held at a local church the following week, though we needn't feel pressured to make the journey; he was "all right." About Htet, he added nothing.

It was Nora, a few hours later, who filled in some of the rest of the picture for me. I hadn't told her of my recent estrangement from Charlie, maybe for fear she'd confess to things that would cause me to see his sudden departure

147

from the rooftop restaurant in a new, distressingly clarifying light. Had he only indefinitely walked away from me that night, or also from his family? And if the latter, had he left for someone else (for example, her), or to pursue that will to wander that had so vexed and enticed me? I hadn't wanted to know.

Of course, since my rupture with him, Nora had mentioned Charlie during our own few visits—something about a book he was reading or a subject they'd discussed—so that I understood they were, at the very minimum, corresponding. Yet I was startled when, soon after receiving Charlie's message, I called to break the news to Nora and she responded, "It's devastating," as if she'd already heard from him. And then: "I've been meaning to ask how you're doing." When I pressed her about what she knew, she explained that Wah had ventured into the fire-engulfed house next door to save a homeless teenager, a boy who had perished along with her and who had probably started the fire inadvertently, though on this point, she said, Charlie had been vague. "How can he not feel responsible?" she added about Charlie. Responsible because, according to her, he hadn't lived with Wah since Christmastime. I knew that, didn't I?

What I knew, even then, was that my guilt ran as deep as those other feelings that made me suddenly want to defend the woman who in life had maddened me.

"I hope you haven't been sleeping with him," I said into the phone, before a protracted silence on the other end of the line led me to think that Nora had hung up on me.

"You really have a low opinion of him now," she answered finally, in that restrained, deliberate way she has. "It's not like that, Mom. He's suffering. We're friends." She could have gone on: *I've been suffering, too, and our friendship has been a solace to me.* But she said, "He's in love with someone else, anyway."

I think it was to honor Joaquin as much as Wah that I soon made plans to fly out alone for the service. Milton had gone through his own moment of reckoning after we'd received the news; sleepless and weak, he seemed to be holding his breath before determining how to proceed. Then something inside him visibly let go, appeared to gasp, as if he'd decided that only the idea of Wah—or the ideal of devotion and service she represented—had held any true worth for him, as opposed to the flesh and blood substance of the person she'd been. "I think I'll let you attend the funeral without me," he announced over dinner on the night after the news came. He's a decent man, Milton, but he's even more ruthless than Charlie if you look at him a certain way.

I'm not sure what I expected to discover at the service, what I most feared; possibly a horde of students and do-gooders weeping over Wah's casket, or else that other woman, the one Charlie supposedly loved, standing faithfully and unsuitably by his side. Maybe because Charlie had organized the affair or because the direction of Wah's devotion ran nearly exclusively to Htet, hardly anyone was present. When Charlie immediately offered up a speech (strangely focused on the ways he'd failed to live up to Wah's expectations— "She wasn't one for artifice, so I'll tell you honestly that for a lot of our marriage I felt like I wasn't good enough for her"), it was to no more than a dozen souls, among them several members of Wah's extended family from the looks of it; a dazed Ernie, flanked by a pair of elderly women I'd seen on his porch from time to time; and Duane, who sat apart from the others in the rear and looked so heavy lidded and hollowed out that I would have taken him for Wah's lover had I known nothing of her death's circumstances. The fire having occurred on his neglected property must have weighed on him terribly.

Htet sat alone at the front with Charlie, armored in the same provocative garb by which she seemed to dare you to cross her. Yet she wasn't all aggression that day. When a hymn started up, she lifted her voice so that I could hear the heartrending strains of her grief from where I was sitting. And listening to her, and watching waves of emotion breaking over her face, while beside her Charlie stared at his open hymnbook as if to hold it responsible for his pain, I seemed to glimpse not just the extent of her aloneness now but also the triumph of her continued life.

In the reception hall after the service, Charlie was too shocked or shamed to speak more than a few words to anyone. Nor did I observe, among the others present, any conversation about either Joaquin or what had occurred to cause the fire in the first place. At one point, I turned to find Htet staring at me across the echoing space with the strangest look of regret, but she glanced away when I began to approach her. Even Duane seemed to want to evade my expressions of dismay and sympathy, responding to my questions concerning Joaquin (and where and to whom I might pay my respects) by saying something clipped about the young man having already been laid to rest. For a moment, he studied me with a sort of questioning blame, as if I'd been the one to start the fire or to steal Charlie from his family. Of the actual new woman in Charlie's life, there was no sign.

No sign, at least, until six months or so later, when my marriage and writerly productivity had reached their lowest points (in contrast to my drinking's new heights), and when Charlie wrote to say that he was in the city with a "friend" and wondered if he could come by.

So it was that in late August, a little more than a year after his first visit to the farm, he pulled up before our porch in another rental vehicle and waved to us through the heat before skirting around to open the passenger door for his friend—Melyssa was her name—while I was taken back to the experience of meeting him as a stranger, when the handsomeness of his face and the cleanness of his smell had convinced me that Milton and I had no reason to be wary. We are what we choose to recognize, as much as we are what we choose to see. Or: we are what we are capable of perceiving. And how heartbreaking it was to look down the driveway and perceive an old friend in a new, meaner light.

For an hour or two, the four of us sat in the Adirondack chairs by the pool, sipping on something cold that Milton had poured out as Charlie introduced us to Melyssa. I'd already expected her to outshine Wah in certain ways, but only then did I realize I'd also expected her to more closely resemble me. She was young, she was pretty. She moved her shoulders and the head on her neck with a sporadic flirtatiousness that suggested someone was repeatedly tickling her spine. She heaped praise on Charlie without a hint of criticality, though she claimed to want to write.

"You *do* write," Charlie told her protectively.

Aside from her credulousness, I didn't like the uniformity of her speech, or the symmetry of her hair's layers and highlights, or the shape of her eyebrows and lips, perfected to give her half-frozen face a perpetually sardonic sultriness. Nor did I care for the enhancements peeking out from the deep V of her T-shirt's neckline. Yes, this is a record of meanness and, I admit, perhaps also one of anti-feminism, of how merciless women can be in scrutiny of one another and of how far we may go to prove ourselves enough to be liked. Melyssa's efforts were only more glaring than mine—and paid for, it seemed, by the husband she was now trying to divorce, whose own gargantuan efforts at self-enlargement (or -enrichment) had recently taken a disastrous turn. At least, that was what I inferred from Charlie's aside that the legality of the nasty prenup her now bankrupt ex-husband had made her sign was presently being raked over by her team. It was all so prosaic and disappointing.

Still, I felt sorry for Charlie. He might have been better off as Don Juan, after all, with a string of temporary loves that included me. But he had found his corner, a more appropriate and diminished one, and more ordinary, if ordinary takes as its measure not just the mores of the day but how most people are capable of behaving. Watching them together, I was reminded again of the close presence of the boy in the man. The restlessness hadn't left him; when he shot a glance at the hedge trees over his shoulder, I seemed to see someone long accustomed to attacks on the person he couldn't help being. Or maybe I was only reading myself into his story. He put a supportive hand on Melyssa's back—to steady her against my scrutiny, I thought, or to brace himself against the incessant tides of his shame. I suppose he hoped we would forgive him for everything.

And Milton seemed intent to do just that. He kept refilling their glasses, laughing about a joke I'd missed, sending frightened, darting glances my way, no doubt afraid I'd skid off the path of this rocky reestablishment of our camaraderie.

"How's Htet?" I asked.

That hand on Melyssa's back: I saw it give a little rub, as though to knead away the knotty problem I had raised.

"How about we talk about it another day?" Charlie said with a blink.

"I feel bad for her," Melyssa announced. "Some nights I wake up just—" She shook her head, as if to shake off the horror peeping out from behind the curtains of her immobilized face. Yes, it is easier to condemn a woman, particularly when she has something we lack. "I don't think she liked me."

"*Liked?*" I couldn't understand her change of tense.

But Charlie was done with my interrogation. "Can we talk for a minute inside?" he said to me, standing from his chair and dusting off his jeans. "I want to ask you about how Nora's doing."

He didn't sit when we entered the shade of the kitchen, just pulled up in front of the farm table and stood as though readying himself to tell me something important. Yet it wasn't of Nora that he spoke, nor of Htet or Wah or Melyssa, even.

"Did you tell your editor to reject me?" he asked.

154

An instant passed before I oriented myself to the direction he'd taken—to the book about masculinity he'd conceived of with my editor over dinner following the awards ceremony.

"I have no idea what you mean."

He studied me, as if to assess the extent of my dissembling. But I didn't really understand. My editor had never said anything to me privately about Charlie. I told him as much, and after a moment, I saw that he half believed me.

"Maybe I was too honest about my ambivalence in what I gave him," he said.

Honest about the constraints of domesticity for a "masculine" man? I wondered. About the constraints of monogamy? Oh, Charlie. How much he was like Sisyphus, who for his blasphemous passion and self-interest, and for his disregard of the gods of his time or their moralities, paid the ultimate price: a sentence to infinite ineffectualness.

"I told him about Htet," he went on, sinking into a chair as if in defeat. "I tried to describe the way it feels, to meet your daughter when she's already formed, already harmed by men, and someone capable of looking at you with profound skepticism. If I'd known her before the damage, if I could have prevented it, protected her as a little girl . . ."

He turned his searching gaze up to mine, almost to invite me to finish his sentence. But I didn't know what to say. I didn't like his assumption of victimhood or the implication that his affair with worshipful Melyssa could be justified by

Htet's judgment and inattentions. As far as I knew, his grown daughter's "skepticism" could have been born from a growing awareness that his attentions were straying from her mother to other women, including Melyssa—and me.

"It was like looking into a distorted mirror, living with Htet," he said, "and constantly seeing my flaws exaggerated."

"Sounds like a real relationship," I said. *Unlike the one you have now,* I didn't have to add.

He must have seen it in my expression—my allegation that he'd swapped one child for another—because he said, "I do care for Melyssa."

It wasn't so much the words as the aching tenderness with which he'd spoken them that convinced me he was, indeed, in love—not with Melyssa, necessarily, but with Wah, with the dream she'd tried to cast and that he'd failed fully to believe in. But I don't think he could allow himself to see it that way.

"This isn't just infatuation with her youth," he tried. "Some crisis of midlife, of perception—isn't that what you call it in your book? The 'midlife crisis of perception.'"

He set his eyes on mine, so that I saw he meant to convince me of the reliability of his perspective, to persuade me to keep my faith in him and our friendship. And staring back into those feeling, guarded eyes, I *was* almost persuaded. I seemed to have arrived at another crisis point, one from which I saw, at once, the trustworthy man before me and the helplessly lost one within him. It is perilous to feel for those whose loyalty and insecurity so seamlessly coexist; it is perilous because they never stop being and not being what they appear to be. They defy categorization like escape artists. But aren't we all some mix of truth teller and phony, devil and saint? There is no safe love. Only *safer* love.

"So what now?" I said. "You do the cliché thing and start another family with a new woman? Start all over only to see it again, the same looks of skepticism and disappointment? You can't escape being disrespected, Charlie. Not if you're unworthy of respect."

A flicker of something, anger or pride, coursed through his face, and I thought he was going to shout at me, or pull me finally into his strong embrace. But he said, "No." And then, "Maybe." And a quivering smile spread over his mouth, so that I feared he would start laughing, something that made me afraid I might do the opposite.

"What about Htet?" I managed.

There it was again, his look of defeat. "She's gone," he said.

"Gone?"

"Back to Malaysia."

I asked him what in the world he meant by that, and he began to explain—with no shortage of head jerks—that the girl hadn't wanted to live with him after the funeral and had moved in with Ernie, before her therapist and several social workers had convinced him that she should be allowed to return to the convent for a time. "The *convent?*" I asked. And he squinted at me as if to suggest that we'd already covered the subject during our various conversations. The last place Htet had resided in Kuala Lumpur, he clarified; where Wah and Htet had met, and where previously—after the girl had been rescued from her traffickers and bounced between various terrible juvenile shelters—a nun had taken her in, the same one now serving as her temporary guardian.

And so, Sister, we finally arrive at your entrance into this story.

A minute passed as I stood there, taking in the extent of my friend's abandonment of his child. It wasn't indignation I felt so much as a desire to blame him for the guilt on which his crime indirectly shone a light. Mine. Yes, it was just as I described near the beginning of this confession, a feeling of being a little animal bounding for a dark hole in which was buried her own guilt. But there was no way to bury that guilt still deeper in front of Charlie. There was no hiding.

"You can't just *abandon* her," I told him.

"I haven't *abandoned* her," he insisted, and I saw in his face that he believed what he was saying.

"But it's your chance—" *His chance?* Even then, my point escaped me.

"My chance?" he said, reading my mind more perfectly than I. "To come through finally? She's too smart for that,

Tessa. She *sees* me. I don't think she even *blames* me. I've never been her parent, not really."

How convenient that he had the excuse of having adopted her at a late age, not to mention his *masculinity*, to exonerate him from that mandate to try, at least, to be a parent and for the duration of his child's life. And what *is* a parent, finally? The person who puts in the time? Or also the person whose attention—in light of the one known as "child"—isn't overly co-opted by other sights?

"Are you all right?" Charlie asked, and I saw that he was watching me with pain.

"What did you want to tell me about Nora?" I asked him.

He frowned, but whatever displeasure or confusion he felt soon enough melted into a look of worry. "I guess I wanted to ask if you thought she'd want to stay in the house during her breaks," he started. "I can't sell it—not with the burned house next door still standing. Can't face it. And I thought it could be a free place for her to figure things out. Or you two—"

It was "two" he'd said, not "too," I soon realized, though he could be so careful about the way he put tender things.

"You and Nora," he went on. He must have noticed the trouble Milton and I had been facing. "If you want to spend time there, alone or with her. She talks about you all the time. 'Mom' ... 'Mom' ... It's always right there. You."

13.

C AMUS SAYS THOSE WHO LOVE TRUTH must seek love in marriage, "in other words, love without illusions." So what does that make me, the lover of reality who hasn't managed to abide by her marriages' realities: A champion only of my own version of things? Or, at least, of how I want things to be?

It was while Milton entertained Charlie and Melyssa out on the patio into the late hours of that August afternoon, their laughter echoing off the pool water in which I liked to swim, that I began to pack up my life. And it was a few days later that Milton made his confession to me about Kathleen. I've already mentioned the start of that conversation, I mean when I came down to the kitchen to find him boiling pasta and drinking water (as if to simultaneously steam and flush me from his system), and I asked about his first walk with Wah on the beach, and he said they'd spoken of "the call to serve," how he'd thought if he could "just soldier on like her" we might survive. Is it always like that, with someone who gives too much and another who takes mercilessly? A tale of martyrdom and narcissism, or a tale of love and temperament—which one is this, would you say?

"I've been talking to Kathleen lately," he added then. "Phone calls. Texts . . . I don't really know what's going on. If it's a reaction to us or . . ." Or *the start of something*, I understood he meant. "It's been a relief not to have to pretend anymore that the boys are a less important part of my life." *Less important than you.* "I think it's possible I still love you, Tessa. But not to the exclusion of them. That's something Kathleen understands."

How strange that he was getting to this only now, after all his posturing about the joys of freedom, and after real freedom had come with the boys' independence. And all along I'd thought we had been making the mutual, rational choice—like the one parents are instructed to make with airplane oxygen masks—to prioritize our own vitality.

Ernie was on the porch when I pulled onto the block the following month, having driven myself across the country alone for the first time. If before the Victorian had been something you had to turn your eyes away from in shame (too plainly had it displayed the record of its former inhabitants' hopes and defeats, their fanciful and insular origins, their doomed

162

Mid-City fate), now the charred ruin spoke only of . . . well, ruin. But I couldn't comprehend the reality of lives being lost to it any more than I could grasp just why I'd felt compelled to stage my disappearing act here. I stepped out of the car and raised a shaking hand to Ernie, who offered me an unexpected smile, so that I thought he must have survived the street's various iterations—not to mention his own relocation from it during the war—by similarly screening out what he preferred not to see. And as I opened the lockbox and proceeded to heft my bags up the walkway past his gaze, I grasped that I represented another iteration, one the old man might be taking comfort in, as I was no victim of circumstance. Not really.

Dumbly, I stood with my things in the stagnant element of the Craftsman's interior and then thrust open the windows and went out back to take stock of the garden: its eastern hedge trees alternately singed and dead, its ground strewn with ashy bits of timber and strips of burned paint, and its view now dominated by the eerie spectacle of a three-story brick chimney looming—scorched and unsupported—over the Victorian's collapsed backside. Soon enough, I retreated into the house, furiously evading reminders of the woman I had tormented: the blue ceramic teapot in which she'd steeped her reedy tea (and which I replaced on the counter with a jar of coffee grounds I'd brought west with me), the banker's lamp in the living room (now tucked into the linen closet because I couldn't face the other closets or the bedroom that had once beckoned to me), and so on. Htet would want her mother's things, I told myself, making mental note of my trail of concealment, though I couldn't *really* think of the girl, no more than I could face the actuality of Wah's or Joaquin's permanent absence.

That night, I slept in the guest room, or tried to, willing myself not to long for Milton and waking with a start whenever a helicopter or firework sounded in the sky. I told myself that what I'd conveyed to Nora over our strained exchange of emails had been right: that although I was leaving Milton indefinitely, my stay in Los Angeles would only be as long as the time it took me to figure out what, if anything, I still wanted to write. Yet I seemed also to be avoiding any confrontation with the idea of writing as the days began to pass—arduous days, filled with disorientation and doubt and physical aching for Milton, whose voice I kept anticipating as I staggered around with my silent phone in hand. Why exactly had I left him without a fight? And why had he ever loved me—*if* he'd loved me? And had I *really* loved him, if I was actually *capable* of loving?

It was during those days of stupefaction and remorse that I found I had a harder time overlooking my invasion of Wah's territory when it came to certain utilitarian objects I'd never bothered to see: the cabinet's smudged glasses and chipped plates, nearly every drawer's crumb-strewn lining, the stained towels, the dingy sheets . . . Of course, I'd been confounded by Wah for as long as I'd known her, yet I hadn't doubted her scrupulousness before; as I've said somewhere in this, there was a harshness about the scarcity of her furnishings that I'd attributed less to her want of money than to her love affair with deprivation. Now I wondered how scrupulous she'd really been, whether the scarcity and griminess on evidence might not have had more to do with the hard truth of her limited means.

That feeling of double vision—of remembering how I'd seen things and seeing them again in a vaguely different way—was with me on an afternoon about a week and a half after my arrival, when to escape my discomfort in the house I ran out for groceries and returned to find a small gathering of neighbors under the flagpole on Ernie's lawn. One of them, a woman I'd glimpsed at the funeral, cast a friendly smile my way, and when I crossed toward her, groceries in my arms, I saw that Ernie was sitting on his porch above us, observing me with interest as a portable CD player spooled out a recording of Bing Crosby's "White Christmas."

Her name was Shirley, the woman told me. And I was Tessa, right? She'd seen me around—nobody's business was just their own on this block. She laughed, and for a while we talked amiably. I mentioned that "White Christmas" seemed an interesting choice for October, and she explained that

Ernie had first heard the song when he'd been a boy with his mother in a camp. A perfect song, it had seemed to him, a song that still gave him hope. It was his birthday today, she added, nodding at Ernie across the lawn. Eighty-six. They'd known each other for more than forty years, since she'd moved to the block with her husband in the '70s. She gestured to a large yellow house on the corner, where she'd raised her boys. But when I made a comment about it being idyllic, her expression darkened, and she began to speak about the day, a long time back, when her husband had headed out the front door on his way to work and been killed during a shooting. "We're all right," she went on. "My boys are strong. The youngest, Caleb, is still living with me. And Ernie and I check in on each other all the time."

The depths of her eyes lingered questioningly on mine, so that I thought she was waiting for me to respond, but none of the words my mind inwardly settled on seemed remotely sufficient. Caleb had been the one to spot the flames, she said, and another moment passed before I understood she'd leaped to the more immediately wrenching subject of the fire. Whoever had wanted that house destroyed had done a good job pouring gasoline over its second story, she went on. The flames had spread fast. If Caleb hadn't called when he did, Wah's place would have been completely overtaken. I must have looked dumbfounded—it was impossible for me to believe that Joaquin or Duane could have had anything to do with arson. "Charlie didn't tell you about the damage to his property?" she asked. "Everything had to be taken out and professionally cleaned. Windows on the east side blown out, siding singed. All of it replaced. Weeks passed before any of us could process it—we were all reeling, trying to help with Htet. But eventually we came together to work with Charlie's insurance and a contractor." I asked if the contractor had been Duane, but she shook her head. "That man probably wants to put up a high-rise now," she said. And then, as if to prevent herself from elaborating on ugly subjects: "I hope Htet will come back. She should be living here with Charlie. He's a good soul. Cares about that girl, whatever people think. I just pray he finds *himself* someday."

A few mornings after the neighbors began to take down their Halloween decorations, I woke to a rumbling, and shielding my mouth and nose against a cloud of dust outside, I soon found Shirley and others congregated across the street as massive demolition equipment encroached on the Victorian. Many of the neighbors were recording what was happening with raised phones, so that they seemed to be steeling themselves against the destruction by means of the distancing mechanism of their screens. And I was probably steeling myself with the punishing thought that if I'd never told Wah that Charlie wanted to leave her, he might have stuck around and prevented the fire from happening. He could have been there to save her, at least.

What got me as I stood guiltily watching with the others was the water, the way the crew members shot enormous plumes of it up into the air—thirty, forty, maybe fifty feet—as a measure against the dust, someone explained. And as a measure against everything that house had harbored, I thought: all the loss and terror and pain, all the madness, poverty, greed, despair, inequity, loneliness, pride, cruelty, and suffering. All of it washed away. A few of the neighbors said what a shame it was, lamenting that the house might have been saved. It occurred to me then that nothing should be saved at all cost, that the house's time had come. Though when I glanced west and saw Ernie's empty porch, I understood that even with his failing ears, the old man must have been hearing the collapse of something as real to him as anything in his eighty-odd years of life on this street.

For a while, I retreated inside, to the nook off the living room and the secretary desk where I am now writing, from which I could peer periodically through the shutters' slanted slats at the neighbors still gathered outside. I tried to concentrate on something I meant to read, but instinct kept drawing my attention to the window, and soon I saw Duane sitting behind the wheel of his parked truck up the block.

He was gazing toward his property and didn't seem to notice when I began to cross toward him outside, though several neighbors watched as I skirted the demolition scene. The crew had already started in on the foundation. Maybe because of all the pounding, Duane started when I rapped on his window, so that for a moment all we could do was stare at the surprise of each other through the glass, absorbing everything that had come to pass, or so it seemed to me.

Did he want to come in? I asked with a gesture before covering my ears against the noise.

Ten or fifteen minutes later, after I'd removed myself from the neighbors' watchful stares, he was at the door, looking so ashen and distracted that it seemed redundant when he entered unprompted and sank into one of Charlie's seats.

"What brings you back to the inner city?" he said, as I brought out some hot tea. "I'd have thought someone like you would do anything to keep away from here."

I should have had something biting or corrective to say to that. Instead, I seated myself across from him and told him I'd left my husband and taken up Charlie on his offer of time at the Craftsman.

"The Craftsman? You mean this place?" He gazed around with an expression of bewilderment before his eyes returned to study mine. "Sorry to hear about your marriage. Always a reason to go. Almost always a reason to stay. I told Charlie that, but he didn't want to hear it."

"You're married?"

The question seemed to surprise him nearly as much as it did me. "I was." He nodded in the direction of the thudding next door. "That house was supposed to be a new beginning for me." Again, he took me in. "How did you manage to do it, leave a whole life?"

I couldn't seem to proceed in this mode of personal revelation. "Charlie never mentioned your wanting to move into the house. I thought you were going to fix it, sell it off."

"That's what he said?" His expression didn't change—he was still studying me intently—but I felt the heat of offense rising to the surface of his stare. "I don't know what everyone around here has against me. I guess you heard the rumor I burned down my own place. Meanwhile, my insurance won't give me a dime because some jerk found an empty gasoline jug in the rubble. That could have been left by anyone. Or been sitting up in the attic for decades, the way that hoarder lived."

"The woman who owned the house before you?" *A woman alone*, I remembered Wah telling me. *A woman left alone with her duty.* "Why didn't you clean out the house after you bought it from her? You have to see how it looks, your leaving the house to rot on this street. Making it so easy for Joaquin to break in and hurt himself—or worse. *Anyone* in his position would have lit fires."

"Fair enough," he conceded, his attention straying to the wavy-glass window facing the view of Wah's singed trees and the demolition beyond. "Sometimes I think it's retribution. Twenty years chasing money, turning over properties, never a hitch. Or almost never. I came in with a partner and started flipping during the crash. People losing everything . . . It takes a hard heart to face a man who's crying because he knows he can't hold on to the place he thought would be his family home forever." He glanced at me as if he thought I would commiserate. "I should have kept to lath and plaster, my first line of work. My father and I used to come into places just like this, make them perfect—and I don't mean uniform like everyone wants these days, smooth without an impression. See that shadow?" He pointed to something on the ceiling I couldn't see. "That's what you want—a bit of imperfection, variation. Whoever did this job knew what he was doing." He pushed himself up and ambled to the stairwell, where he craned his neck to gaze up at the second-floor ceiling. "I always wondered what the inside of this turret looked like. Just by the coving you can see this isn't a pure Craftsman. Beautiful joint work. Plastering couldn't have been easy."

Pure Craftsman—the phrase confused me, and when he turned around to face me, I asked him what he meant by it.

"People get lazy with categories," he said. "Makes them feel they have control, mastery. I don't have to explain that to you—you're a writer, right? That's what Wah told me."

The mention of her name caused a change to come over him. I felt his openness begin to fall away, and I was sure he'd find some excuse to leave. But he didn't move yet. He said, squinting at me across the distance, "You ever read her book?"

With embarrassment, I confessed that I hadn't. "Not more than a few passages online."

He nodded, as if he appreciated my honesty, and said, "She seemed like a victim. And I'm not saying this to get myself off the hook or anything. But knowing her, reading what she wrote in there . . . It's like she *wanted* to die."

14.

I N THE HOURS after Duane left, I wandered around the
house touching its contents, as if to make contact with
traces of Wah: her special wineglasses that we had held to
our lips; the dining table that she had set and cleared for us
on so many nights . . . I had come to distrust my perception
of such things since my conversation with Shirley. Had those
plates in the cupboard been chipped by the remediation
team? Had neighbors, as untidy as they were helpful, left the
crumbs I had wiped away from the kitchen drawers? It may
seem silly, but these questions nagged at me; I seemed to be
trying to wrest the truth of the person Wah had been from
the mute objects before me. Only later that evening—when,
for the first time since living in the house alone, I braved the
bedroom she had shared with Charlie—did I grasp the futility
of this effort. The stripped bed, the bare desk, the closet's few
remaining articles of clothing, the damaged garden outside,

the cleared plot where just that morning the Victorian had stood—it was all so different from the reality that Wah had known here.

And yet wasn't it *her* reality that stopped me, as I turned to leave the room and saw—among the piles of books that someone had put on the shelves where she had kept laundry—my own book, *Midlife*? Wasn't it *her* reality I recognized in the heavy marginalia scribbled on almost every one of its pages—not in Charlie's childlike lettering, but in a practically illegible cursive that slowly began to translate itself to me as Wah's?

It's not quite true, the idea that, like Sisyphus, we toil and get nowhere in our lives. Or if it's true, then the impressions we have made, the perspectives we have held, still have the possibility of eternal transformation when taken in and reconceived by others' eyes. I found it almost dazzling, the difference between how Wah had seemed to me in life and how she came off in the margins of *Midlife*, which—even as I crouched on the corner of their mattress—I began to reread through the prism of her consciousness. *"No recognition of bias,"* she had jotted down by the title of one of my chapters. *"She is one kind of maternal pain, I am another. Me, sacrificing too much. Her, too little."* Here was the opinionated Wah, the Wah who felt free to diagnose, to read fiercely into things. *"Maybe by believing in her, in her code of self-interest, Charlie justified his inattention to Htet,"* she wrote at the conclusion of a passage on Don Juan that Charlie had several times told me he liked. And then: *"But he is <u>exactly</u> the kind of man she would leave."*

This Wah made me view the other one—the Wah I'd known—as a muzzled woman, biting back the bile of her life to accommodate people's idea of her as docile or decent or just exceedingly polite. And *this* Wah seemed to recognize the disconnect between my own outward presentation and inner existence: *"Chasing after reality all her career, and why?"* she scrawled beside one of my paragraphs in which the word "reality" appeared like a pinball, ricocheting wildly through the sentences in a way that embarrassed my now distanced editorial eye. On another page, she had triple underlined my phrase "the unreality of my childhood." I'd forgotten that particular wording and, by means of her emphasis, saw myself suddenly as the riddle I appeared to be for her, perhaps as much of a riddle as she had been for me. It caused me to drop the book and retreat to the room I was staying in, carrying with me a sensation I'd had as a child—the feeling of being as unreal as my stuffed toy rabbit, whose worn edges I'd held between my lips each night in order to fall asleep.

It must have been past midnight when I returned, sleepless, to Wah and Charlie's room and ransacked its shelves in a desperate quest to find *her* book. But it was just like Wah, wasn't it, not to keep a copy of that in the house. Or maybe Charlie, out of cowardice or pain, had hidden it away, his wife's story of the girl who had come to define the family he'd left.

Well, you can imagine my fright, my feeling of having at last lost my grip on reality, when, heading out the door the next morning for a run, I spotted Wah's book beneath the porch mailbox. It turned out Duane had left it for me, along with a note of thanks for the tea. *"Tell me,"* he added in his own compelling hand, *"if you see what I'm seeing."*

What I saw, as I read the book out under the acacia tree and then on the living room sofa when rain forced me inside, was the surprising frankness with which Wah described Htet's rage. She writes that she herself had come to the convent— yours, Sister—as part of a larger study that she was then conducting on domestic abuse shelters in Southeast Asia; yet what had led her to your door was not just your order's calling to help the women and children most afflicted by life and outcast by society, but also its emphasis on reconciliation. How might reconciliation square, she wondered, with the kind of wounding that left one on the brink?

It was a question that began to be answered for her when she met you and Htet at the convent. At Wah's first evening meal in the refectory, after everyone sat at a long table, Htet stood, took her plate, and sent it sailing into the wall behind her. Wah was taken by your composure as you sat at the head of the table, waiting for the commotion to die down. You asked the girl to come to you, and then you held her hand and said, "Later, I want you to tell me what is really troubling you." What was really troubling Htet, Wah would learn from you, was the profound unfairness of what she had already endured in her brief life: how she had been born in Burma to a single mother who routinely beat her; how her closest family member had been the little brother who'd chased after the Malaysian traffickers to whom her mother sold her; how by the time she'd arrived in Kuala Lumpur as a girl of six she'd been sexually assaulted; how she was subsequently locked in a basement with twenty or more other children who were starved and beaten when their days spent selling knickknacks on the streets didn't yield enough money; and how she had learned to love—*love*—the woman of the house, whose affection she courted by becoming the child with the best returns.

"This didn't stop the woman," Wah writes, "from continuing to beat Htet." Just as, apparently, it didn't stop Htet from continuing to believe that what she'd shared with the woman had been love. During one of your counseling sessions with Htet, Wah observed you impressing upon the girl that love didn't look like starving or hurting someone, that "*love protects*." And in a singular moment of self-revelation, Wah shares her own thoughts about love—not with you, Sister, but with the readers of her book: "I didn't tell Sister that I understood where Htet was coming from. How can anyone else say that what she experienced with the trafficker was not love? It could have been a certain form of love, however flawed. A love lacking the usual boundaries. We want everything to look the same: this is healthy, that is toxic. But sometimes people can only love as they love. And some of us are stronger than others, better equipped to endure the damage that comes from a damaged heart."

Better equipped to endure the damage that comes from a damaged heart?

To *whose* damaged heart might Wah have been referring? She seems to want to return to the subject a few chapters on, in a scene of her wandering into the convent's chapel to find you, Sister. You were sitting on a bench, and she assumed you were absorbed in prayer, but you turned to her with an interested smile, your discerning dark eyes taking her in. You asked if there was something she needed, and she told you that she had been pondering your adage that love protects. Htet's trust in you was obvious to her, she said, as was the way you returned that trust with tenderness. Yet she'd also seen Htet raging at you—how the girl cursed and called you names after breaking that window in your study, how she rebuffed you when you bent to help her pick up the pencils that she'd been using while learning to write. Was it not true, Wah wondered aloud, that you loved Htet at the expense of showing yourself a protective love? And was it not true that Htet loved you even as she abused the peace you granted her?

I admit that reading this, Sister, I experienced a sort of anxious contentment. Wah seemed to be poking holes in the cult of Christian simplifications you represented. And yet, she also appeared to be justifying something again, some cult of her own, one that took as its central, outrageous tenet the notion that damage—perhaps even abuse—did not forbid love. Maybe you sensed this, too, or else felt what Duane would: that residing within Wah was an instinct for self-destruction. She describes you frowning very briefly before you said to her, "It is a matter of limits. I am here. Htet is there. There is no question of her rage doing me harm. No question of my using her rage to punish myself. It is her own self-punishment. And she is learning to reconcile herself with what has been, to see that she is worthy of a life without self-harm." If Wah doubted that she, too, was worthy of such a life, she never tells us; for the rest of her story, as she becomes increasingly responsive to Htet's suffering, she avoids any mention of the state of her own sensitive heart.

The rain had ceased by the time I finished reading her book, and for a while I stared out the living room windows at the trees whose slick leaves gleamed in the fading day. It seemed to me that I had mistaken the rain for a presence—something capable of connecting me with Wah beyond the grave—so that now, in the immense quiet, without the company of that melancholic droning, and without the company

179

of Wah's hesitant words on the page, I felt acutely alone. It occurred to me that Wah wasn't so different from the women whom she had researched for her book. Or rather, that the primary difference between her and them had been a matter of limits, to use your phrase: whereas they were surely seeking an end to domestic suffering, she appeared to imagine herself "equipped to endure" it. No wonder Htet and Charlie had clashed. Whatever hurt, whatever damage, Charlie had caused Wah, the girl would have wanted to come to her mother's defense.

I remember a conversation with Charlie in this house. We were in his armchairs, as usual, and it must have been two or three in the morning, with the others asleep upstairs or at least pretending to be. I asked if he could explain Nietzsche's concept of eternal recurrence because I had been wondering if it was related to Camus's Sisyphus, and he said that it was a test to gauge a person's ability to affirm life. The question Nietzsche posits, he told me, is if a demon were to ask you whether you would choose to live your life again and again exactly the same way as you have already lived it, right down to the last detail—all the good, all the bad, everything ad infinitum—would you accept? Would you say yes? "Nietzsche once admitted he didn't even know if he could answer in the affirmative," Charlie said. "He called it the greatest weight. He'd suffered so much in his life."

I scoffed and told him I didn't like the test, not at all, because it didn't take into account disparities, the fact that some people are born into unspeakable disadvantage and agony, while others are born into disgusting privilege.

"The test isn't about privilege," Charlie said. "It's about *life*. Agony is life. Inequity is life. Why are you privileging privilege?"

He was being absurd, I said. "Do you think your family members who were victims of the Holocaust would say, *Yes, sign me up—I want to do it all over again*? You can't tell me they wouldn't be likelier to fail the test—fail to 'affirm life'—than someone with power and comfort and money."

You can imagine how we fought about that.

Well, when I wrote to you in late November, a few days before Nora came to stay here for Thanksgiving, I was thinking of both Charlie's test—Nietzsche's, that is—and your own point that love protects. I had found your convent online and written to the email address on the contact page. You know this. But what I haven't told you is that I was still unsure what precisely I was seeking when I agreed, two days later, to your request that we meet by videoconference before you considered granting me permission to visit Htet in person.

After my exposure to you through the mechanism of Wah's writing, it was simultaneously strange and consoling to see you on the screen—not unlike the time I first met

Charlie at the farm, now that I think of it. You were so much more casual in your presentation than I'd expected you to be, younger looking, though I felt your similar surprise as you studied my face on the screen, so that my bewilderment was delayed by a second or two when you said, "You are different from the way Wah described you."

It was as if I'd stumbled into a parallel reality. Wah's book, of course, had been written years before she'd ever met me, and for me the reality of you in Wah's life stopped on that book's last page.

"We talked weekly, just like this," you explained. "You were part of her life, and she worried about her life."

"She worried about me?" *About what I was doing to her life*, I did not add.

I'd positioned myself in a corner of the guest room so that you wouldn't see Wah's trees through a window, her living room furniture, the terrain of her life that, like some conqueror, I'd overtaken. I didn't want you to think I meant to make Htet mine, too, though maybe I did. Maybe I wanted to help correct the girl's trajectory and so correct my record of motherhood, or my soul, or only the relentlessness of my days.

"Wah prayed for the strength to forgive you," you said.

"Why should she forgive me?"

"For being you."

I hadn't expected that. "And did she manage it?"

182

"To the extent that she tried." You smiled with that, as if at a little joke.

And to follow suit, I laughed when I replied, "Tried and failed," something you seemed to appreciate.

But a moment later calmness came over your face. You were peering at me intently, waiting for something. A confession of some kind, I feared. Though it was *you* who made the confession: "In the months before she died, she was trying to write a book," you said. "One that concerned you."

"A book that concerned *me*?"

You shook your head, as though to awaken your usual restraint. "I only mention it because it assisted her." You paused, so that I thought you were finished. But then you said, "If writing for you is like prayer for me, you might try to write about what happened, too . . . And you might try to address the state of your heart. Its hardness. I apologize for stating it so directly, but that is what I see."

I must have sat there for an hour after our conversation, feeling disembodied in front of my dark screen, the keen slipperiness of time. Finally, I stood and began a search that took me through every closet and bin and cabinet in this house, until at some maddened point I gave up and went to sleep. When I awoke early the next morning, it was with the realization that I was at last ready to write again. And after descending to the kitchen to make myself coffee, I went to the nook off the living room and switched on the light. Only then, as I sat at the secretary desk, did a shiver of knowing pass over me. I had forgotten to check this desk's drawers; forgotten because—though I'd never dared open them—I already considered the desk mine.

It was all there, several journals and her laptop, whose password was affixed to the lid with a sticky note, as if whoever had stowed it away—Charlie, maybe—were urging me to pry.

"My Nemesis." That is what Wah had titled the folder on the laptop with hundreds of documents devoted to me. Or not *me*, but the Tessa whom she'd simultaneously gotten all wrong and frighteningly right. Even having read her marginalia on *Midlife*, I hadn't anticipated a Wah this virulent, this dark, defensive, mocking, and unhinged. And, Sister, she had begun her project far earlier than you had suggested to me: "You don't have to sentence yourself to duty," she quoted me as saying in a document whose date roughly coincided with my first visit to the Craftsman. And then: "Only someone whose people haven't suffered would say such a thing." And later: "Does it not occur to her that I am also a woman? As if it were a monolith: womankind." And maybe worst of all: "How is it that Milton knew about Charlie's affair and she didn't? She, with her firm grasp on reality?"

The poison of her disdain. I thought I couldn't read another line, but, clicking through the documents, I found some reassurance in the gradually changing tenor of her voice. "Maybe I *am* a weak woman," she ventured around the time she must have told you about her writing, when things in this house had perhaps settled down somewhat after Charlie's abrupt leave-taking. And later: "Try to see yourself as *she* sees you, in order to see yourself more clearly." And then: "I think she recognized how alone I am: alone with Htet, never enough money; because *she* is alone." And later: "What do I really want with this? Retribution? Or to love her. I *admire* her. In spite."

It was with a sort of melting feeling—of sorrow and regret and something I couldn't name—that I began to read the notes she'd started taking in the weeks before she died, notes for a novel told in third person, in which I was "Larissa" and she, "Khin." But Larissa was so much more powerful and alluring than me, and Khin so unexpectedly aware, even in her supplicating positions:

When they met, Khin kept smiling apologetically at beautiful Larissa. She felt caught between a desire to make a joke about the mess of her own life and a fear of igniting her husband's ire.

His attention to Larissa was rapt, devotional. He couldn't seem to help himself. Powerless before the queen.

Larissa was dressed in torn gray jeans and a sheer linen top, so that Khin could see her fatless, strong body beneath.

Dangerous, Larissa's conviction. Convincing. And daunting. Like a current of electricity drawing people's attention her way.

Glancing at Khin, Larissa waited for her to finish making one of her intellectually starved points.

A tentative girl came out of hiding in Larissa's face whenever she laughed. It made Khin want to protect her.

Larissa wanted to slap Khin. To slap away the look of weakness she never wanted to see in the mirror.

Something terrible infected the air between them. They couldn't speak two words without becoming sick with the threat of their differences.

On and on it went, these efforts that seemed to verify and recast my experience of what had been, to throw us into humiliating and sympathetic relief.

And then one day, toward the end of a page of false tries, she hit on something—an idea for an opening line:

When Larissa accused Khin of being a disgrace to women . . .

Well, I have given you my own version of the rest.

So it began, Sister, this address to you. My days, rolling the boulder up the hill, doing battle with my hard heart, trying to commit to the page my own truest confession of what happened, feeling as though I've made headway—then falling back. Nora has twice come and gone in the interim, and, as far as things stand between us, little has changed. "The struggle itself . . . is enough to fill a man's heart," Camus says of Sisyphus's predicament—an idea I've tried to comfort myself with.

I might as well confess here, since I've been too shy to do so during our weekly dialogues, as you call them, that Duane has recently become my friend. Ernie watches when we walk around the neighborhood and then when Duane follows me in. We're not going anywhere, Duane and I. We're not getting anything done together—not the elaboration of ideas, not the creation of new homes, and certainly not our divorces. But he shows up, or I call him to me, and we struggle to exert ourselves on each other, to expend whatever needs to be expended. And he goes away and shows up again, or I ask him to come, and we repeat.

Someday, when I trust myself not to bring up the subject of his American flag, or his policework, or his "White Christmas," I'll go next door and properly introduce myself to Ernie.

"I want you to know," Duane said before he left the house last week, "that I think you are a trying woman." Naturally, I took this as a misogynist statement because of its implication that I'd failed to meet a certain standard of agreeability to which only women are held accountable. "That's what I mean," he said when I told him as much. "You're *trying* to do right, but everything's *wrong* by you. Still . . . I'm drawn to you." After I'd thought about that for a bit, I decided to forgive him.

The other night, I made him some dinner, and we sat in my dining room, I mean Wah's (and soon to be someone else's: Charlie has said that any day he'll put the house on the market, though when I make noises about packing up, he begs me not to leave yet). Maybe because I'd made some effort with the meal and set the table and lit candles so that there seemed to be something sacred about the ambience, Duane took his cap off before eating and held it in his hand and bowed his head. And I sat there, watching him in judgment and wonder—half reading his thoughts, half realizing

I'd never be able to read them—willing myself to say some of the words you had sent to me as a prayer. But it didn't work. I couldn't force myself to believe in it, your prayer. The act felt too imposed, the words too artificial in my mind.

And yet, I imagine it's not a lie that what I've been doing these last months with this manuscript is similar to prayer. Lately, I've been meditating again on the question of femininity and motherhood, and I've found myself thinking of the way Camus described his mother, who was deaf and nearly mute. In his writing, she is always impossibly beautiful, inaccessible, passive, compliant, a sort of Cinderella doomed by poverty and disability to scrub others' houses and watch in helpless grief when her children are subjected to the blows of injustice. In other words, she is the epitome of the feminine ideal, but not the *maternal* ideal, for in a sense her solipsism betrayed him as a child. She was everything, and she was utterly unattainable; and it is tempting to blame her for Camus's subsequent ravenousness for women. It is tempting to say something like: the condition of motherhood is a tragic one, for to be self-interested or self-contained is to doom one's child. But I reject that out of hand. Look what became of Wah.

When Camus died, he was forty-six and had already been publicly condemned for his political and philosophical moderation. He was still married, having just holidayed in the French district of Yonne with his family; yet he was also privately reeling from rejection by a lover. The immoderate moderate, we might call him. Well, they had been joined in Yonne by another family, that of his friend and publisher, whose own immoderation soon sent them zipping in the man's sports car back toward Paris. "Is it really necessary to rush?" Camus asked this friend before the car swerved. Among the wreckage was Camus's valise, its contents including Nietzsche's *The Gay Science* and a draft of his own autobiographical novel in progress, *The First Man*, whose publication would be suppressed for decades.

And so it goes: the boulder up the mountain, the heart thudding and skipping down. A soft, unclean wind rustling through the branches. Marvin Gaye singing of inner-city blues on my phone. On better days, I ask myself what more there is than just this. Wah's things, soon to be packed up and stored, or sold, or left for someone to claim—maybe I will be the one to claim them. Ernie's swing songs, drifting over his fence to the place in the backyard where I jot this down. Yes, on better days I sense something like a thought joining together everything that has ever existed. Maybe Nora will come for another visit. Maybe Duane will stop by tonight. Maybe Milton and I will find our way back to speaking.

You must see it all the time, in your haven for the trafficked and the abused, in your teen self-respect workshops and family reconciliation sessions: the almost comical way we humans crash into each other, reel back, and crash again, as though what we really want is to be broken by the very thing we mistook for love. As though we just can't stop punishing ourselves for our errors of perception.

Or maybe they aren't errors. Maybe what we called love was love. A certain form of love, as Wah wrote, to which narcissism or fear or a lust for justice all at once blinded us. Maybe Camus had it right, that truth can only be found in the disillusionments that come with something as intimate as marriage, to which he himself couldn't be faithful. So what does that make us, Camus and me and someone like Charlie? Fantasists like Don Juan? Or only people who need, now and again, to seek refuge from the reality of their lives, the truth of themselves?

"There are those who can't keep sight of themselves and those who can't keep themselves out of their own sight"— that is what you told me a few days ago, after you sent me the words of another prayer, one by which I might appeal for the strength to leave myself, if only for a moment, the better to see the condition of my heart. I didn't tell you that, throughout the writing of this account, I have been working on just that, trying to keep Wah's perspectives in mind—all her notes, all her scathing critiques—never taking her words for my own or violating my sense of truth while writing, but asking myself where I might be blind, such that sometimes I can no longer claim to know where in this I have expressed merely my initial impression and where that impression has been enriched by her mind. And yet, it seems to me that this story is realer than anything I have yet written.

And so I put down my laptop and look out over the field where the Victorian stood, its weeds worrisomely tall and brown. And again I try to say the words that you sent to me.

Give me the strength . . . Give me the strength . . .

Like pebbles, they are almost unbearably hard in my mouth.